About

C000246466

Adam Vincent is a stand-up comedian and writer. He has no other skills. There was a five-year patch where he became a nurse for the money, but getting into nursing for the money is akin to becoming an accountant for the vibe, that is, it's ridiculous. After realising the error of his ways, Adam made another questionable decision and moved his family from sunny Australia to Bedford, England. The move paid off as he went on to spend ten years as a core writer for Channel 4's satirical comedy show The Last Leg which has been nominated for both BAFTA and Rose d'Or awards. This is his first novel.

If you would like more information on Adam, please visit: www.adamvincent.com

How **Not** to
Kill Yourself
When Living in the
Suburbs

Adam Vincent

How **<u>Not</u>** to
Kill Yourself
When Living in the
Suburbs

Pegasus

A CIP catalogue record for this title is available from the British
Library

ISBN 978 1 91090 392 6

Pegasus is an imprint of
Pegasus Elliot MacKenzie Publishers Ltd.
www.pegasuspublishers.com

First Published in 2023

Pegasus
Sheraton House Castle Park
Cambridge CB3 0AX England

Printed & Bound in Great Britain

To Nicky,
we said we would and we did.
Thank you.

Acknowledgements

Craig Barfoot started it by getting me drunk and suggesting we both have a crack at writing books. So thanks Craig and thank you beer. Thank you to Nicky T. for reading draft after draft and always providing great notes. This book would not have been possible without your guidance and humour. Thanks also to Grainne Mcguire, Dan Gaster, Paul Revill, Alex Brooker and Dean Griffith for your positive and constructive feedback.

I must thank my children. You're too young to read this yet but one day you might and if you do, just know that I think you're both the most brilliant and inspiring kids a dad could hope for. Now go and make something of yourselves.

To Mum, Dad, Nathan, Carina and Kirsty, while distance and the cost of airfares keep us apart, you're always in my heart and I'm forever grateful for your support. I promise to never spend birthday money on bills again.

Big thanks to Pegasus for taking a chance on a no name like me, and to Joe Norris and Ruth Gladwin for helping me with the fine print.

And finally, thanks to the real Judy, your resilient positivity and wicked sense of humour never cease to amaze.

Children, put this book down now. This is my zone, mine, not yours, mine. This is where I spew out my darkest hopes and insecurities, and it's not for the likes of you. So back away. You get everything else: my time, my money, my love and adoration, my will to live, but not this. And the way I see it, if you are reading this, it means I'm either dead or you're rifling through my drawers. Either way, I expected more.

If I am dead, just know that I did my best. Yes, you were born with Australian passports and yes, you were raised in Bedford, that's on me. We all make mistakes and your biggest mistake will be reading any more of my journal! Trust me, you'll find no answers here.

Your dad shits once every two to three days and it's never an easy shit. That's the kind of sentence you're going to read. Honestly, if Instagram stars knew that I was looking at them mid strain then placing my phone gently in my underpants to wipe turd smears off my arse grapes, they'd probably stop trying so hard.

I warned you.

Now if you're someone else's kids, I never liked you. Ever! So read on, you noisy, phlegmy little bags of other people's responsibility. I'd like nothing more than for you to realise what your parents have had to deal with.

If you're thinking of starting a family, treat these pages as a guide to what not to do.

And if it's too late and you're already dealing with all the emotional detritus that comes from having your own brood, then sit back and have a laugh, as I'm sure you're making a better fist of it than me.

I keep waking up at four a.m. wondering how I'm going to pay for it all. The mortgage, the bills, the never-ending need for shoes, the always wanting meals, the after-school snacks! How much do these fuckers eat? Nobody tells you that your children will need to be within three feet of pre-packaged carbs at all times. My two are insatiable. They're like rabid dogs who'll bite your face off if you don't throw them a treat. It's literally crackers. Our last Aldi run was a hundred and forty pounds! These buggers are five and ten! The teenage years will break us. I've run the numbers. The only way I can retire is if I die at fifty-eight. And even then, the kids would still have to leave home at sixteen, Lucy would have to get a better job and we'd have to sacrifice a room to a lodger, but this way we keep the house. I will have to rest comfortably on the mantlepiece. I don't expect a high-end vase, a shoe box will suffice or they can put my ashes in an old tuna tin. Don't wash it out, fish oil will help conceal the smell.

Fifty-eight!

It's three in the morning. The birds aren't even up yet. I woke up before the fucking birds.

My maths was wrong. The only way I make it to fifty-eight is if nothing changes, but in maths, the variables always change; that's why they're called variables. How could I have been so stupid? I'm a stand-up comic who barely scrapes by, nobody knows me, really I'm a part-time stand-up comedian and full-time delusionist. These are not the best foundations to build a fifty-eight-year life span on. It's remarkable that I've fed us for this long. Last week I drove to Exeter for a hundred and eighty quid. Six hours of Friday night peak hour traffic there, four drowsy hours on the M5 back. I spent fifty on fuel, four on a sandwich and for what? A hundred and twenty-six pounds profit and the chance to be yelled at by a drunk farmer? Not worth it! I have to break through soon or I risk having to get an actual job.

But what job? Retail? Truck driver? The robots are coming. For an unskilled grafter like me, comedy may be my best bet. But the road, it's so brutal. I often don't get home until three a.m., my arse numb from the drive, shoulders aching, and my bladder ready to burst but there's never a car space available. A terraced house might look good but our lack of a driveway is going to cost me a kidney. It's getting dangerous. I often find myself having to park six streets away which is an impossible journey on a full sac. And taking a slash behind a neighbour's bin is getting riskier by the day. I'm an Amazon door camera away from seeing myself on the street's Facebook group, "Anyone recognise this serial pisser?"

Last week I emailed Harry asking for writing work. It was Lucy's idea. She often tells me, "You're very funny on paper," which my insecurity translates as "You're rubbish on stage." But financial insecurity is the strongest of all my insecurities so I touched base with Harry and today it paid off. I think. It's hard to know with Harry, he's the best-worst comedy agent in Britain.

"I hear Bournemouth loved you, Adam, you're on the up."

"I've done that gig eight times now Harry, the only thing I'm on is antidepressants…"

The second most infuriating aspect to Harry is his use of the word luck: 'As luck would have it', 'Today is your lucky day', 'Unlucky about the misplaced cheque but luckily I can post you another'. In his world, I'm a black cat away from signing on. Obviously, his most annoying trait is his use of cheques. We live in a world where cars can drive themselves yet Harry refuses to get off parchment. I can't leave him either because, unluckily, he has cancer and one of the first rules of showbiz is you can't leave your agent mid-lymphoma. That's frowned upon. That he's had it for eight years now and that some suspect he actually suffers from Munchausen Syndrome is also a detail worth considering. I have my suspicions. He's too chipper for terminal and he's an absolute unit. A six-foot-tall tubby cancer patient eight years into a diagnosis? I smell bullshit, but how do you bring that up?

"Harry, I think you are sick but more in the head than the blood." What if I'm wrong and he actually does have cancer? No amount of luck would get me out of that one. Until then, he gets fifteen-percent of everything I earn, which isn't much.

Sometimes though, he does get positive results.

"Well your luck is turning my friend because I read your email requesting some writing work so what did I do? I hopped onto LinkedIn Premium is what I did, and guess who has a trial writing day for TV?"

"TV! You're taking the piss. Which show? What channel?"

"The shopping channel!"

"The shopping channel? Seriously what is it?"

"That's it, the one and only, a guy called Glen reached out, he's a fellow Australian and if he likes the cut of your jib, he tells me you'll be on thirty quid an hour; lucky you. Anyway I'm feeling a bit rough and need to lie down, doctor's orders, I'll email over the details this afternoon."

One of the perks of having 'cancer' is you've always got an out to the conversation and Harry uses this to full effect.

'A guy called Glen...' Astonishing.

━━━━━━━━━━━━━━━━━━

Harry emailed the job brief, it was short and to the point, 'Need jokes about absorbent mops'. Legal wants us to avoid the words, 'moist, wet and dirty', lawyers take away all the fun.

I'm not above writing gags about super absorbent mops, so I googled that fellow Australian 'guy called Glen'. The internet tells me that Glen Farmer is a middle-aged madman stuck in the eighties, and he's come out of nowhere and struck a chord with late-night losers. He's 'on the up' as Harry would say, so it might go somewhere. It has to.

I pitched them the line 'squeaky clean so you don't have to be' and then inserted the direction of a double pump of the eyebrows with the suggestion that Glen talk dirty to the mop, but the notes were it was too avant-garde. Instead, they liked 'Did somebody say Mops? Because we've got mops! Mops! Mops! And more mops! We've got mops coming out of the wazoo! Get a mop for your mum, buy two for your dad, that's right they'll even wipe away misogynistic stereotypes'. Like that but worse.

What have I become? At one point in my life, I wanted to be an engineer yet here I am desperately hoping my mop jokes work so I can get paid to write more. We all suffer from spells of low confidence but to lose sleep because you're worried someone is out there writing better mop jokes? Talk about tragic. It's like having imposter syndrome with a bucket of shit. Ironic that a good mop joke might clean it up.

━━━━━━━━━━━━━━━

Day eight with no sun. There is a definite correlation between me not getting vitamin D and me creating problems that aren't there. I have loads of actual problems, overdue bills, chronic neck pain, no work, no savings and the kids need new school uniforms. There's enough to be getting on with. Yet my brain thinks the best way to avoid real-world problems is to create imaginary ones and then see what happens. My latest is I have a deep-seated worry that Lucy will leave me for some financial adviser, probably called Greg, who works in London, earns mega wads and has a massive cock. This Greg prick always takes out the bins, he's good with the kids and a demon in the sack. They'll probably meet in the park, he'll be walking his dog, which will be a King Charles Spaniel because he's a prick, it'll get loose and run to Lucy who'll find it adorable.

"Bjorn seems to like you, usually he doesn't like strangers," says Greg with his charming Nordic twang. Their eyes meet and immediately there's an attraction. Lucy will try and fight it, but his calm demeanour is too alluring. I'll do my best to win her back but it's hard to beat such a well-heeled figment. Hypothetical Greg, he earns. I see it perfectly. He showers my kids with gifts and stories about his time as a sea merchant and they lap it up. 'Till death do us part' more like, 'Till Greg rocks up wearing his responsibility pants', I see it, man. They sit by the fire while Lucy cooks them all dinner. Then the kids go to bed and Greg bangs her senseless. Afterwards, they hop online to look at holiday destinations in the tropics. That's how it goes. I spend the rest of my days stinking it up here alone in Shitsville as Gregory moves my family to a fjord side ski ranch just outside Oslo.

"Fuck off, Greg!" I said that out loud on the footpath like a crazy person. There was no one around me called Greg, just two dog walkers who quickly crossed the street. I've never even met a Greg.

Eight days, no sun.

Experimenting with happiness:
I've developed a system that seems to be working, kind of. I get up in the morning and stomp around the

bedroom yelling 'I love Bedford. I love Bedford. I love Bedford'. I thrust my hips back and forth, humping my way across the floor boards, shagging the morning air in a frenzy, chanting, 'I love Bedford. I love Bedford. I love Bedford.' I'm desperate for my neurones to wire themselves into a position where I can experience a modicum of joy. This morning, after a few laps of the bed and with Lucy in hysterics, I open the curtains to see what the day had to offer. Drizzle. It's always drizzle. A grey windy drizzle that makes you want to cry but you dare not, as the last thing this town needs is more drizzle. The old me would've shut the curtains and slumped arse first into a pity-party but not today. Today I doubled down. I stomped harder, chanted louder, 'Bedford! Bedford! Bedford! Love! Love! Love!' and the hope is, that one day, I will actually believe it.

━━━━━━━━━━━━━━━━━━━━

This made me laugh. Our local rag, The Clanger, is full of gloriously biased facts. Two years ago they brought out an article saying that Bedford was voted the most generous town in the UK. It might be true. Our butcher regularly gives the kids a free slice of salami. Only when Lucy is buying, of course, prick. Marg, who runs the corner store, is also more than happy to spot you if you are short of change. It's only a quid here or there but it qualifies as generous. What cracks me up is last week,

The Clanger ran with the headline 'Bedford – Voted the most depressed town in the UK'. Isn't that a hoot? What a turnaround! I'm sure I played my part. My facial expressions alone would've got them into the final. But I love the dichotomy. You never know what you're going to get in Bedford. It could be someone offering to help you carry your groceries, it could be someone falling on you from a building. It's that kind of town.

I always wanted to move to London. That's where the adventure is, the action, the hubbub, the brouhaha, the late nights and the big ideas, the poor man's New York. That's what we signed up for but unfortunately, the commuter town of Bedford is all we could afford. Nothing says, "You're not living your best life" like moving to a town because *in just thirty-five minutes*, you can be in a better town. Ah, Bedford, it's like standing outside a window and looking in on an orgy, you can see the fun, you just can't touch it. And that frustration was only ever meant to last for five years. 'Five years and we'll reassess' is what I allowed myself to believe. Idiot. What I didn't consider is in that five years I'd get heavily involved with a mortgage, we'd have another child, they'd both go off to school and I'd spend the remainder of my days wondering how I became completely ensconced in suburban drudgery. No one wants to be ensconced. It's dull.

I try and be positive about my life decisions but whenever I tell people I live in Bedford they react like I'm trying to put my penis in their ear.

"Bedford? You left Australia for Bedford?" Their head jolts back to avoid my verbal cock, as my shoulders slump forward acknowledging the error of my ways.

But what can I say? Lucy has my heart. If my wife wants a pram-friendly town with good schools and no excitement, my wife gets a pram-friendly town with good schools and no excitement! The fact that she had enough cash saved for a healthy house deposit may have also swayed my opinion. It was a mutual decision but she did have all the money and the vagina and I'm a sucker for both. No doubt I will soon be properly depressed again and suggest we move back to Melbourne, the poor man's London, but it will go for nothing. I have no power. As much as I love and adore my family, I'm a bit like Fiji at a climate change meeting; no one cares what I actually think.

It doesn't help that our house sits in the shadow of the Bedford prison. An actual prison! We had no idea. We were impressed with the schools and parks which is real estate jargon for 'safe but boring' but you convince yourself that maybe that's okay. Maybe boring is what we need right now? Then we walked down the oak tree-lined river, noticing the beautiful parks either side, crossing a bridge that's literally called The Butterfly Bridge, and it all felt so Tolkienesque. If you squint you could be in The Shire. It looked like the perfect town for raising children. Then we discovered that Bedford had a shop called 'The Cheese Shop' and it looked like it might be okay for adults to live here too. How hard could life be in a town that had a store dedicated to offering up the world's finest Gorgonzola? We were sold. So three months after our first visit we poured our life savings into a money-guzzling pile of Victorian bricks with big cheesy dreams of a good life. And then, after a week of unpacking, we popped out for a family walk to see what was what. And there it was, only four streets away, a massive fuck off prison standing right in the middle of town, Mordor.

I couldn't believe it. You know what really brings out the bleakness of drizzle? Curled razor wire and watch towers. Had we just taken one look on Google Earth, we would have spotted it! Idiots! No amount of Stilton can justify such a calamitous error. Not that we could buy any because six weeks after moving in, the Cheese Shop closed down. What a turnaround, one minute you're thinking about opening a wine bar, the next you're worried about a White Supremacist called Dave tunnelling his way into your lounge room. I see it happening. His head pops up in front of the TV as we watch another repeat of Grand Designs.

"I'll be hiding out in your rafters until the heat dies down. Anyone calls the bizzie and they start drinking Redrum, comprende? Stop looking at the swastika on my forehead! Now tell me, what's for dinner?"

Lucy doesn't share my Comprende Dave concerns. She can't believe a prisoner would be stupid enough to go through all the trouble of escaping prison only to hide two blocks away. I tell her that Comprende Dave has never played by the rules, that's why he's in prison. If the cops think he's half way up the M1 then his best chance is to hide in our rafters and if we don't leave soon this theory is bound to play out. I've put this argument in my portfolio of reasons to move but Lucy doesn't comprende.

Living in a depressed town that has a prison in its centre is like living in a Turducken. You know where they cook a chicken inside a duck and the duck inside a turkey? That is my world. Solitary confinement is the chicken, the cell block is the duck and Bedford is the turkey. It's confronting. We're all doing time in one form or another. You make small talk with other parents in coffee shops,

"What are you in for?"

"We moved for the schools and the parks. You?"

"I killed someone."

"Really? Who?"

"The young *me* who wanted to move to California and maybe one day get his own Netflix special."

At least the prisoners know that they'll be out on parole in a few years. I'm here for life. Outsiders drone drugs into the prison. At least they've got that. No one is droning drugs into my back garden. And as for shower sex? Ha!

They must have liked my mop jokes because I got another day writing for Glen. He called me himself. "I don't deal with fuck'n agents," he said. I lived in Australia for most of my life but I've never met anyone who sounded more Australian than Glen. He makes me sound French. He is a proper Outback Australian. Bum-fuck-nowhere-hiding-from-the-law Australian. A voice that sounds like a chainsaw fucking a cockatoo, Australian.

"Mate, I need fuck'n six rip roar'n lines about fuck'n screw drivers. She's got a fuck'n Phillips head and a serrated shaft that'd slice a fuck'n wallaby out of the jaws of a hungry fuck'n dingo. You got me? Fuck'n work from home on this one, the Mrs is over from fuck'n Thailand and she's hornier than a fuck'n bucket full of bulls. But listen, if I can shift a few thousand of these bad boys then the channel are look'n at fuck'n given us a permanent eleven o'clock slot. So, when you can, cunt!"

In Australia, if someone calls you a cunt it means they like you.

"Righto, Cobber," was my response. I haven't called someone 'Cobber' since I played Ned Kelly's brother in my high school play. That's the problem with the Australian vernacular, it's competitive. One bloke says 'ripper' you have to follow it up with 'bonza'. If your mate says 'his mouth is a desert', then yours has to be 'as dry as a dead dingo's donger'. If I'm going to start working with this Glen bloke then I will have to remember how to speak Chainsaw.

I have no idea how Glen got to the UK, how he started working on a late-night shopping channel and how he hasn't lost his job swearing. All I know is he's now paying me two hundred and eighty pounds a day to write jokes for late-night TV. It may not be for The Daily Show but Glen Farmer presents The Shopping Shed is going straight on the CV.

━━━━━━━━━━━━━━━━━━━━━

Lucy and I went out to celebrate the new job by getting a coffee and having a walk in the park like we used to in years one – two BC (Before Children also Before Cellulite, Before Car-payments and Before Crying).

I forgot how funny she is. I forgot how completely besotted I was by this woman. I forgot how I struggled to speak. How when she finally agreed to our first date it lasted for fifteen hours. How the second date was twelve hours after the first. How could I land such a beauty? It made no sense then and it makes little sense now.

I spent the first six months of our relationship convinced Lucy was a robot. She was a robot and I was on a game show called Will Adam Fall In Love With a Robot? I half expected people to rush into my one-bedroom flat laughing, "Adam, you big idiot, she's a robot. We put cameras in her eyes. Everybody has seen your vulnerability, it's hilarious!"

No one can make me laugh the way Lucy can. Back in BC times, she'd regularly have me keeled over. She could mimic anyone that needed mimicking. The deaf postman, the lady at my local cafe who always forgot my name, my mum, her mum, me. My God, she does a great me. Especially when I take life too seriously. Within a year of us dating her giant-cranky-oaf work was impeccable.

And wasn't BC life full of glorious nothingness! We swooned in the nothingness.

We'd think nothing of drinking too much wine or smoking too many cigarettes. We'd think nothing of going to the theatre and talking shit with wankers who called themselves artists. We thought nothing of sun kissed weekends down at Sorrento beach, nothing of sneaking into the Gin Palace and pretending we were millionaires, nothing of spontaneous shags in the hallway, nothing of a quick trip to St Kilda for sunset and pizza, nothing of walking through the Fitzroy Gardens to smell the summer rain, nothing of picnicking on the Yarra and cheering on the suits as they cycled home from work. We thought nothing of sleeping in until twelve, reading the paper until two and having breakfast at three.

We thought nothing of fun.

Now, everything needs a meeting or a consideration or a budget or a babysitter. And yes, in hindsight it could be argued that we should've spent all that free time in our childless years focusing on our careers so that when we did settle down, we wouldn't be living on the bones of our arse. But, God, we would laugh.

And it's days like today where I get to celebrate/make fun of myself, for landing a gig that lets me write jokes for late night infomercials, while walking with my still gorgeous wife, both of us in a thoughtless stupor but still brimming with love and laughter, well, days like today are perfect.

Never again will I live in a semi-detached house that lets you hear people have better sex than you. Of all the days for the neighbours to make a ruckus. A fuckus ruckus! Three times in the same afternoon! Um, excuse me, I have a deadline on screwdriver jokes!

I miss Bred and Tender. They were the owners of next-door when we first moved in. Their real names were Ted and Brenda, but we got bored. Bred and Tender were everything you want from neighbours when sharing a paper-thin firewall. They never had a beef with us, they rarely argued with each other, Bred was happy to rotate bin duties and above all, they weren't sexual screamers. That they did bang was surprising given they were in their seventies. Most evenings around nine you'd hear the springs of their mattress bounce up and down, the odd bit of wheezing and then it'd be over. Their prowess was impressive, and while I try not to be competitive it was nice knowing we could match them stroke for stroke. That is, until last Christmas when Bred actually had a stroke, which was tragic, but it did mean we could finally relax. He was putting in a five-shag week at seventy-two. What a machine! Ironic that he ended up attached to one. Sadly, a month ago, I read his obituary in The Clanger. So now he's Brown Bred. Ha! I shouldn't joke. Poor Tender has moved into a retirement home around the corner. Life goes on. These houses have seen more than us and will see more again. Terry and Jen are just the latest incumbents, and we've already renamed them, The Ice-Screams.

Terry and Jen changes to Ten and Jerry, which moves to Ben and Jerry, which gets us to ice cream, and given they are screamers it's perfectly logical to name them the Ice-Screams. And they are giving us a headache because they are noisy fuckers, literally. Hard and loud! We'll never keep up. They have no kids so it's not a fair fight. I can't remember the last time we had a mid-afternoon romp and they're doing it three times in the one session. It's very disturbing and incredibly distracting. I know when they're going to cum, I know when they're cumming and I know when they're cumming again. The second coming may well be divine but the third just sounds greedy. The irony of listening to screwing whilst writing screwdriver jokes isn't lost on me.

I emailed Glen my lines. He'll probably go for 'That's not a screwdriver with a serrated edge. This is a screwdriver with a serrated edge!' which will crush my soul. I prefer 'like a groom at the end of a busy honeymoon, it's got a serrated shaft' but that might be more of a reflection on yesterday's working conditions than anything. What a stupid job, I feel guilty getting paid to write such frivolous lines but then I look at my bank balance and realise I'm several screwdriver jokes short of being able to afford a tool box, let alone keep up with mortgage repayments. The good news is Glen emailed straight back, 'Beauty, mate!'

I responded with, 'No worries, Knackers,' and he's already put the money into my account. Who am I kidding? I'd wear a cork hat and a shark tooth necklace if it meant making a living.

Last night I was violated by Lucy and I'm not convinced it was in a good way.

At around five o'clock, as the sun set on a rare child-free day, I was encouraged to drink a pint of delicious amber fluid. My feet were up, John Prine's Summers End came over the speakers, I was completely lulled. That should have been my first warning. Normally my instinct is to not trust comfort. When I was six, I got trapped inside a sofa-bed. Ever since I've been suspicious of all things cosy. I should never have let my defences down.

Somewhere between five-thirty and six, a magazine was placed on my lap. It had thick glossy pages and was more pictures than words. I remember hearing murmurs of 'Bronze taps! Quartz worktops! Underfloor heating!' but can't remember in what order these verbal punches struck me. Just after six, someone knocked on the door. I tried to call out for help but I was still reeling from the barrage of pictures and words. The lights were dimmed and plates appeared on the floor in front of me. Had they been there the whole time? It was hard to know. Before I could fathom what was going on I was being spoon fed Biryani. Chunks of garlic naan were dropped into my mouth. This was quickly followed by more of that silky liquid gold. I struggled to resist. It must have been ten minutes later when my belt buckle was undone. Lucy raised her eyebrow suggestively. What was going on? Were we going to give the neighbours a run for their money? It all happened so quickly.

With a burning sensation growing in my knees and Vindaloo between my teeth we heaved across the lounge room floor. I was a hot mess, confused, surprised, happy, discombobulated and finally exhausted. Ten minutes later I woke up from the sex coma with my pants around my ankles and mint sauce splashed over my legs. Lucy was sitting upright watching a home improvement show on the TV and an iPhone, showing off Britain's hottest high-end stoves was held an inch from my face. I was being two screened. That's when the severity of the situation really dawned on me. Lucy was in the throes of asking me to cough up on a new kitchen. 'Bifold doors would really open up the garden and...'

I tried to shut it down but who was I kidding? It was over as soon as she said, 'Bifold'. You don't bring up a bespoke double-glazed panelled window that uses a tracking system for a smooth glide on a whim. This 'chat' was planned weeks in advance. I was dead before the poppadom's had even arrived. What started as post coitus cushion talk about bringing more light into the back half of the house, soon evolved into a 'chat' about the possibility of a hand crafted copper splash-back. My mind was bombarded with images of happy families standing next to new kitchens on polished concrete floors. But they weren't polished concrete floors, they were tiles that were made to look like polished concrete. I pointed out that they weren't really happy families either, that they were made to look like happy families but my cynicism was blunted by poorly timed indigestion. Or was it perfectly timed? The evening had been meticulously planned. I never stood a chance.

This morning, grappling with a raging hangover, I

stubbed my toe on floor samples that had been left in the kitchen. We must have really gone for it. Coloured charts of matt finished paint were stuck to the walls, a space for a potential island bench had been marked out in gaffer tape. Chalk sketching revealed where the new windows would go. She'd even cut out a tree from a magazine and stuck it in one of the corners to give us an idea of the new view. I spent most of the morning running over the night before in my head, *did I promise her anything I couldn't deliver? Overhype the prospects of me making a living from screwdriver jokes?* And then I saw a hammer wedged into a wall that separated the kitchen from the breakfast room. I remembered yelling, 'If you want a bigger kitchen, baby, then let's get you a bigger kitchen because daddy's earn'n'.' We mixed Indian take away, with beer and sex and then hopped online YouTubing home improvement shows before knocking back half a litre of Smirnoff. No good could come from this. What have I done?

———————————————

I have decided that I am going to plan my own night of persuasion. Obviously, it can't have anything to do with sex. I have moments in the sack but shagging my way out of a white quartz worktop with copper trimming seems like an impossible task. I'll have to be meticulous. I can't copy her methods. A takeaway

Vindaloo would contradict any suggestion of financial vigilance and while my culinary skills are OK, much like my penchant for cunnilingus, they can only move minds so far. It's clear that I will have to use more nefarious tactics. The gloves are going to have to come off, or in this case, be put on. I will have to clean. I may not be able to shag my way out of a new kitchen but I can clean my way into the possibility of keeping the old one. Tomorrow, I begin, Operation Cheap Bastard.

Operation Cheap Bastard

Phase one.

I have enrolled the kids into a tennis camp for this weekend. They'll be gone between ten and four which gives me six hours of quality manipulation time. It's a forty-pound outlay and the kids have no idea how to play the game but every war has innocent victims and sacrifices must be made.

I went to the supermarket and stocked up on cleaning products. They're hidden in the boot where the spare tyre used to be. The spare tyre is now hidden in the side alley. I told Lucy the alley was infested with spiders and that she best avoid. Perfect.

———————————————

Lucy keeps questioning me about flooring. I've had to bite my lip a few times now. I must stick to my game plan. To bow out early on a, 'But our kitchen works fine', would be a suckers move. I'd never recover from the arguments that would follow plus she'd double down on the trickery. Banging the drum about, 'living beyond our means', may feel like an honest and open approach but it's a fool's errand, an impossible task, I have to try and outsmart her. I secretly plot as she discusses parquetry. She probably thinks I'm disinterested. I am, it's boring as hell. Herringbone is for losers.

———————————————

I just discovered a hidden cupboard full of cleaning products. I'm not sure if they've been there all along or if Lucy is attempting a similar move.

———————————————

Disaster!

I've been told that the kids will need to bring their own tennis rackets to tennis camp. All-inclusive my arse! Once again, I've been scuppered by the fine print. I suggested maybe they include a hand-ball class. Declined. The cheapest new rackets I could find are forty quid a pop! And guess who sells them? The same man who runs the tennis camp. This bloke is in the racquet racket. Borrow rackets? I've asked around, no one we know plays tennis. Why would they? It's a dork sport.

———————————————

Had a boozy business lunch with Glen in Dulwich. Twenty-eight pounds for a return trip that doesn't include the Tube. You head in to try and better your life and it cost you three days' worth of gas and electricity. Thieving arseholes! Wasn't all bad though, Glen's been moved to the eleven p.m. slot and wants me as his right-hand man. He brought me in to discuss his plans.

"We're going to fuck this wallaby, mate. You hear me, cunt? With my energy and charisma and your fuck'n weird ideas we'll take this town! Now let's sink some piss and make this official."

Translated that means, 'I'll have work soon but first I want to make sure you're not a complete prick!'

I think that's what it means anyway. I'm tired, drunk and a train ride poorer than I was before I left this morning. Plus all that money I spent on beer! Glen had better come through with the work otherwise this boozy business lunch was just a boozy lunch and I can't afford those. Especially when tomorrow at dawn phase two of Operation Cheap Bastard begins in earnest.

Operation Cheap hungover bastard.

Luckily my fear of financial ruin trumps a throbbing headache.

I woke up at dawn, popped two aspirin, whipped on the Marigolds and scrubbed like my wallet depended on it. Not a surface was left unwashed. The kitchen tiles sparkled and the grouting was almost mould free, even the ceiling got a rinse. The skirting boards glistened, the carpets were crumb-less and the mantelpiece was clean and clear. I may have failed to successfully screw the cupboard door back-on, and maybe a large portion of the floor tiles remain chipped and risky to cross in bare feet, but throw on some shoes and rub some Vaseline on your glasses and our kitchen is as good as new. I dusted, I buffed, I spat and I polished. By the time Lucy awoke her breakfast was made and our kitchen looked like it was wearing a fresh set of second-hand clothes. Even the hammer stuck in the plaster board was made to look like it belonged. It's now where we hang the calendar. I didn't mention any of my efforts. That was for amateurs.

From Lucy's point of view, we woke up at the same time and I wrangled up some eggs while she was in the shower. Yes, my fingers were raw, my knees ached and my nose hairs had been singed by bleach fumes, but my mind was on point. The waft of bacon was a worthy aromatic decoy from all the cleaning products used. The kids sat and ate their breakfast at the table excited about their tennis camp. And Lucy thought she had mastered the art of subtle manipulation. It was all about the lulling. I gave the kids cheerful dancing Dad as opposed to gruff and grumpy Dad. I made Lucy a fresh cup of tea, left her favourite book on the couch, I lashed out on a fresh bunch of flowers for the hallway and played Morcheeba over the speakers. These little touches may set us back a few quid but as I have already stated, with every war there are sacrifices. After dropping the kids off at tennis camp, I was perfectly placed to begin phase two of Operation Cheap Bastard. It was time for some Netflix and Grill.

Knowing we now had six hours free I suggested that Lucy and I do what we missed the most about our previous lives, that being, nothing.

"Remember when we could afford to do nothing? The Saturday afternoons we used to waste? We used to have such meaningless fun. Shall we?" I jested, pointing at the couch. I knew the answer was going to be a resounding "Yes!" Lucy didn't suspect a thing. It was time to strike. I offered up a documentary that I had been 'recommended'. Of course, by 'recommended' I meant cleverly researched because I am a scheming bastard. We sprawled across the sofa with her head resting on my chest like it used to before the kids ruined everything. Lucy's face was happy and content. She lived in a clean house and had a caring husband who was a loving father. Then, forgive me, I pressed play. Over the course of the next hour harrowing images of the slums of India punched us in the face. The sorrowful wails of crippled children begging for money kicked us in the guts, and the toddlers playing in sewerage knocked us over the head. As if on cue, because it was, an old lady hobbled to the Ganges to wash her dishes. It was a brutal uppercut. Her swollen ankles and rickety legs balanced a container of pots and pans that clanged and clunked on the bones of her aged back as she made her way to an opening in the reeds. I had Lucy on the ropes.

"We just don't realise how good we've got it," I said with a concerned voice.

"I know, that poor lady," Lucy said with tears rolling down her cheeks. I chimed in with, "I just think that if this lady can wash her dishes in a river, surely, we could maybe wash ours in a standard sink? It makes you wonder, do we even need a dishwasher?" This wasn't the final blow but Lucy was on the canvas stunned at what was happening. Her silence meant one of two things. Either she agreed with the sentiment that our lives were already quite good, or, she had cottoned on to my wicked plot. She did have a mind for these types of shenanigans. I had the carpet burns to prove it. I had to push on as if my plan was working.

Round two.

We left India's slums and I decided to switch over to one of Steven Spielberg's all-time greats. Surely no one feels like buying a new gas stove after watching Schindler's List. If Lucy had any empathy, we'd be keeping our old electric hob and saving ourselves thousands. We watched that famous scene with the girl in the red jacket. What a powerful moment! If I played my cards correctly the next morning when I questioned Lucy's choice of a bright red range cooker, she might settle on something a little less expensive. Finally, my Netflix subscription was working for me. We were in tears. Mine were fake of course. Inside I was ecstatic. According to my calculations I was set to save us fifteen thousand pounds. They don't teach this stuff in schools. And I only feel mildly guilty. I'm not a bad man!

Terrible night's sleep, the guilt from my poor form. If you're the future me and you're looking back at what just transpired, just know that we had very good reasons. The biggest being it never ends with the kitchen, never.

Lucy wants these double glazed bifold windows with aluminium black matt finished frames but she never even considers what they'd be revealing.

Pamphlets show pictures of content wives enjoying their morning coffee looking out through amazing windows that reveal lush green gardens. Oak trees and glass houses and Labradors chasing blue birds amongst the morning fog. These magazines are real-estate porn and much like porn I don't have the leverage, be it physical or financial.

As it stands our garden is an artist's impression of abject failure. It's a hodgepodge of broken pots carrying dead plants scattered amongst rotting sleepers. The lawn is more dirt than grass. Crud filled jars and ice cream containers roll around the yard reminding us of happier times when the kids would make potions and shoot water pistols at the neighbour's cat. RIP Tibbles. Rusted dumb bells poke through broken panels at the bottom of the tool shed, heckling me about the time I promised everyone I'd be doing triathlons by June. A rake lays covered in leaves. We've got a dog bowl but no dog. RIP Benji. Our outside broom has a broken handle and rests on the half deflated wading pool which doesn't quite cover the old bicycle that's buried in the ground where the veggie patch was supposed to be. Our garden could easily become a centrepiece at the Tate Modern. It fulfils their requirements, in that it's completely garbage. My point is that any money spent on a kitchen and fancy windows will only lead to more money being spent rectifying this wasteland of despair. Gardens cost thousands to get right but even if we somehow managed to find the money it's still not over.

No one ever talks about the 'showing-off the house' costs. We'll be coughing up dosh for dinner parties for months. All to impress strangers. Canapes made from expensive Italian meats placed on croutons soaked in duck fat. High end fruits being dunked into bowls of chocolate as you hand out fondu forks. 'Isn't this fun?' they'll say while sipping on the wine you didn't want to provide. Jesus, six months ago you thought maybe we could get a new stove but now you're high tailing it to the corner store to buy limes. You hand out mojitos while your wife gestures to anyone interested that the worktop is real quartz. Even if you ignore all the financial pain that led to this kind of evening, there will be no rest because pretty soon you'll be dealing with the reciprocation dinner. Fuck me, where does it end?

You made good on your promise of a new kitchen, you forked out for a new garden, endured months of dinner parties to show the damn thing off and just when you think you're out of the woods, the phone dings. The late night text, 'We need to return the favour'. You attempt to flee the country but it's too late, you've been added into a WhatsApp group titled, 'Dinner Gangnam Style'. Now you're going to be slugged for a babysitter and a bottle of the second worst prosecco money can buy. Not the worst, as that'd leave the door open for accusations of you being stingy. Trust me, the second cheapest is the least best you can do.

Now, if you're not accustomed to the events of the reciprocation dinner, here's how it plays out. You find yourself making small chat with the husband of your wife's friend who she barley knows. This guy hates you because he was ambushed at your dinner party and has just had to cough up for his own new kitchen-bifold-garden-combo. The mojitos that your wife made nine months earlier, really sold it. As an act of revenge, this prick decides to make your home improvements look childish. His kitchen has one of those Aga stoves that runs on smugness, the windows are made from triple glazed high impact German glass, his garden is longer than yours with more girth, but to really smack you in the face with his dick, he throws in a jacuzzi. A jacuzzi which is ready to use. "Fancy a dip?" he asks knowing full well that you didn't bring bathers. "It's OK, we've got spare trunks." What a prick! Am I the only one who sees the real cost in renovating a kitchen? So, judge me all you want future me, or ancestors of my estate who are nosing through my diary, but know that I did what I did because I needed Oscar Schindler to save one more soul or I risked having to share bath water with The Daltons.

━━━━━━━━━━━━━━━━

Two more writing days in the diary is the good news but the far worse news is Operation Cheap Bastard is in trouble. Lucy has booked us in for an appointment at

Sparrow's Kitchens!

Disaster on the school drop off! The guy from the tennis camp got me on speaker phone with Lucy and the kids in the car. Had I just bought waterproof coats we could've walked to school. My decision to wait for the summer sales now seems reckless. When it rains it pours. This tennis coach, Garry Foxe, what a piece of work. He had the gall to suggest Albie had exceptional hand-eye coordination and fast-twitch muscle fibres. 'A rare combination', he called it. He wants me to bring him down to the club next weekend to have a hit with his squad. I laughed at him and politely suggested that he take his business elsewhere and then I hung up. This lead to a big argument with Lucy.

"But what if he is good at tennis?"

Albie piped up with, "I like tennis, Dad."

"So do I," said Lizzie.

I had to fight back.

"'Hand-eye coordination!' Most of Albie's dinner ends up down his front and as for fast-twitch muscle fibres, it's spiffy wank jargon to make gullible parents believe their kids are gifted."

"But what if he is special?" whispered Lucy.

"Yeah, what if I am special?" yelled Albie.

"I'm special too," said Lizzie.

Suddenly everyone was Federer. I had to lay down some home truths.

"Albie, last week you got your head caught in the railing of the stairs. Remember? Your ten-year-old self screaming while I rubbed your neck with butter. And Elizabeth, only five months ago you thought it might be funny to treat the couch as your potty. You're both special, just not in the way you might think."

"You're being horrible about your own children, again," said Lucy, her whispering now on the outskirts of rage.

Albie again, "Yeah, Dad, horrible."

And if there was any doubt Lizzie came in the with a quick jab to the solar plexus, "Disgusting!"

"I love you guys, I do, but tennis is for posh people called Wilfred who wear pink polo shirts and call their parents Mumsy and Dadsy. I'm not going to raise you to be twats. I refuse. Now, if you don't mind, get to your respective classes!"

Lucy trundled them out of the car but told me she would rather walk home in the rain than spend another minute with my good self. She may have replaced 'good self' with 'ridiculous idiot'. Hard to know, as the slamming of the door rang my ears no end.

Lucy enrolled them for a tennis squad!

"What's that Fiji? You're drowning?"

I pulled into the Sparrow's Kitchen's carpark a broken man. We'd just got the quote from Steve, the builder: to get the house ready for a new kitchen; to knock down a dividing wall, put up a steel beam, make space for bifold windows and relocate a boiler was going to cost, all of our savings! And Steve was the cheapest we could find. I couldn't believe it. Everything we had worked so hard for was set to be spent on getting the house *ready* for the kitchen. Schindler had failed me. The Indian beggars only steadied Lucy's resolve.

"I don't want to shy away from a life of abundance," was the sentence that she used. It was over. I had lost. I slunk out of the car, onto the zebra crossing, along the path, through the doors where I waited, ready to be consumed.

"No, thanks," was my instant response when the lady in the blue power suit asked if we'd like a coffee. Coffee never means coffee. It starts with coffee, then you spend the night, then you stay for breakfast. This is followed by children and twelve years later you're sulking to a kitchen retailer on an industrial estate. No thanks. Coffee can go fuck itself.

Like most women from Eastern Europe, Nadia scared the shit out of me. She had a look that was two parts sexy and four parts, 'Many of my ancestors starved to death in a Gulag'. You could see why they hired her. Her voice had the tone of, 'Why would you not want new kitchen? You stupid Western pig!' We sat with her and her computer for what felt like days. There were no windows, no clocks, just kitchens. As far as the eye could see. Occasionally you'd spot another couple in the distance. She was always happy. He was always stifling a yawn.

The three of us spent forty-five minutes deciding between Swamp Green, Robin Egg Blue or Apple Fizz for the cupboards. I didn't even know what Apple Fizz was but I chose it because I wanted the colours to stop. It was like being jizzed on by a clown. This is how they get you. They tire you out, wear you down, degrade you and then don't let you leave. I needed to pee but there were no toilets. The shop next door did bathrooms but why risk more renovations. Fluorescent lighting flickered from above. I was flustered. I think I was hungry. I was on the cusp of pretending to faint when out popped a man from behind a show room larder. Like a Cheshire Cat ready to lead us up the garden path, Rob had a mischievous grin suggesting he knew something that we didn't. Like how much we were going to spend.

"Pop these on..." Rob said holding out two pairs of goggles. "...And get ready to see your kitchen in 3D!" and then Rob disappeared.

It felt dangerous. Like we were set to be sucked into a world that we couldn't afford. My phone had no reception so there was no dialling for help. We put on what looked like a welder's helmet, but it felt more like a blindfold. I didn't ask for a final cigarette. I just waited for the gun to fire. Unsurprisingly, the 3D goggles worked. It was like we were there. The cupboards, the ceramic tiled floor, the stove, the cheap imitation art deco tiles. Goddamn it, the kitchen looked good! And then it happened, the money shot, fired by my own wife.

"I love it!" she cried. Uplifting music started playing from Nadia's computer. The devil himself would've been impressed. The pressure was too intense. I ripped off the goggles and walked outside panting. "I need some air," was my excuse but I needed more than air I needed fourteen thousand pounds and a steady reliable job.

It took a slow walk around the block for me to realise I only had three options. Option one: I could be like those other suckers in the distance, brow beaten and despondent sulking into my sleeves reluctantly agreeing to a shorter lifespan via more debt. Option two: I could put my foot down and just say no. This was the riskiest option as it would leave Lucy distraught and I'd always be a broken cupboard away from losing my marriage. Finally, option three: I man up, walk back into that shop and be a hero.

"We want all of it!" I shouted, striding in with unbridled joy. Uplifting music still played from Nadia's computer but her and Lucy were stunned.

"Even the copper splash back honey?" Lucy asked,

scared of the new man I was pretending to be.

"Especially the copper splash back. I also want the tall fridge with the separate double freezer. I want the handle-less doors that you have to push in to open... And another thing... I want the warming drawer."

"The warming drawer?" Both Lucy and Nadia gasped like I had lost my mind.

"With God as my witness we will never miss-time a Sunday roast again!"

"Promise?" Lucy asked.

"I promise." I was officially crazy. We sat there like two happily married idiots, one of whom still had 3D goggles on. Rob giggled from the ether. Nadia was wide-eyed with possibility. She'd be phoning home about the commission she was making on this deal, that's for sure. There was a tension in the air and I'm pretty sure it was sexual. I was the man. I was, Hypothetical Greg. I signed the papers, I put the thousand-pound deposit on the credit card and then Lucy and I strutted out of that hell-hole looking like we'd just bought a yacht.

Two hours later I was hyperventilating in our toilet, my hands were shaking as I attempted to read the fine print of the contract I had just signed. I had started the month with a humble pot of savings and now I was staring down a three-year interest free loan of over fourteen-thousand pounds that didn't include building costs. Sweet Jesus! Lucy was in the old kitchen making tea to celebrate the new one. As I wiped up what was now vomit, I drew some minor comfort knowing that at least I had this new writing gig. I just needed it to last for another ten years. Am I a fool? The smile on Lucy's face was worth every penny, all one million, four hundred thousand of them. We clanged cups and toasted to new beginnings. It was dreadfully wonderful.

Did another gig in Bournemouth and got home at two a.m., aching. My neck is frozen stiff, so much so that my head now juts out at a forty-five-degree angle. I look like I can't quite hear what the person in front of me just said. On the positive side I did ten minutes of new gear on kitchens and they loved it. I'm hoping this means I can deduct the damn thing from my tax.

Lucy's dad died and she's devastated. Heart attack while he slept, luckily painless. It's terrible news, the worst, and made no better by me.

It's all my fault, not his death but my reaction to it. I never know how to behave in these situations. Not being myself would be a start. I can't believe what I've done. I'm just rubbish at dealing with other people's grief. I once said goodbye to a dear friend who had terminal cancer by asking, "Is your sister single?" And his last words to me were, "Rack off, I'm dying!" Of course he wasn't happy, he was in tremendous pain grieving about a life that could've been but I was so arrogant and insecure that I tried to break the tension. The tension that only got worse when his sister tearfully asked her husband to chase me out of the palliative care unit. But that's my problem, I can't deal with the tension that lingers when death is near.

And I've learnt nothing. Well, almost nothing.

I have learnt that there's a certain amount of time between when your wife's dad dies and when you can introduce a vibrator into the marriage. Now, I don't know what that certain amount of time is, but what I can say is, it's definitely more than three days. In fact, judging by Lucy's reaction, days four, five and six aren't much better.

How do I even begin to explain myself? It's an honest to god disability. Can you claim benefits for ill-timed horniness? Would I get access to disabled parking? A Blue Badge would make driving to the supermarket for a condolence card a lot easier. Aldi's carpark can be a nightmare. Still, the Grim Reaper drawn with a boner might be insensitive next to the car space where they've drawn the person in the wheelchair.

Trying to kink-shag my wife out of despair; what was I thinking? Seeing her there sobbing at the end of the bed yet still wondering, 'Can I turn this around?' What a disgustingly selfish and delusional thought! A late-nineties George Clooney couldn't turn that situation around. I've been rejected plenty of times before in my marriage but I can't deny that getting beaten over the head with the battery end of a silicone wang feels different.

Dominik was a good man. I liked him. He fled Czechoslovakia when the Russians invaded realising early that they would never leave. He then worked hard at making Australia his home, overcoming racism and poverty and never once complaining. At one point he was ordained as mayor of Oodnadatta. What a life! They say he would've made it to Canberra had he not been so successful in business. He ended up travelling the world with his family as the head of a stationary company before settling back to the country that embraced him. Later on in life he succumbed to alcoholism and after investing heavily in real estate around February 2007 was bankrupted by the financial crisis and left unable to leave the very country that saved him. Dominik was a warm spirited man with a good heart and he adored Lucy. After our wedding he was the one who encouraged us to leave Australia and see what the world had to offer.

"I've lived my life, I started with nothing I'll end with nothing but I'll die happy knowing you are out there making the most of every day."

And I bought a vibrator.

The funeral is Wednesday. Judy, my thankfully distant mother-in-law, paid for Lucy's flight back. I protested and said that we could cover it but in truth, it would have wiped us. We're so close to the wire. If the car dies, we're toast. With Lucy away my job is to keep the kids alive for two weeks. It's one of the few times I'm happy I've got nothing in the diary. She flies out tomorrow night. The purple wand remains hidden in my sock draw.

Lucy and I stood on the footpath at four in the morning. A taxi idled behind us with the metre on. Prick. He made me put her bag in the boot. Double prick.

"The kids are going to be fine. Now you better leave. The metre is running."

"Look after my babies."

"They're my babies too and they'll be fine. Everything is going to be as boring and uneventful as it always is. Now you better go."

"OK, I'll call you when I land."

"Say hello to your parents for me."

"I'm flying out for Dad's funeral."

"Yes, you are."

"Idiot."

"Look you're already at seven quid!"

"OK. See you next Tuesday."

"I thought you were back next Friday?"

"*C U* Next Tuesday, remember? We spent last week telling Albie off for saying that to his sister."

"Oh yeah. Ouch! If the plane crashes don't feel bad that the last thing you called me was a cunt. But do feel bad that it cost us 50p in taxi time."

"Well just know that if the plane does crash I want a big expensive funeral."

"I'm just going to tell the kids you left us, it's cheaper."

"If you're not careful, I might."

"I love you."

"I love you too."

The kids are sad that their grandpa has died. They never really knew him as he was always too old and bankrupt to travel from Australia, so they don't know where to put their grief because they don't really have any. They just know they should be sad. Lizzie asked me if I will die. They cried when I told them that indeed I would die, that we all die, that everything dies. Then we started listing all the things that die.

"Trees, Daddy?"

"Dead!"

"Light Poles?"

"Dead!"

"Poo?"

"Really dead! Especially yours!"

God, we had a laugh.

I told them my theory that even death dies. I said when the leaves fall off the trees, that's death and spring is really the death of death. Life is death's killer. I said that Grandpa will probably come back as a bird or a tree or another person, maybe a dancer, who knows. He won't remember who he was but he'll live again, until he dies again and then it'll repeat over and over until he reaches some kind of nirvana state where he moves beyond the life/death cycle. It's around there that I lost them and the conversation was reincarnated into Albie burping the alphabet.

My eggs were a real hit though. Two each sunny side up. I introduced them to Bob Marley, who they loved, and then we went for a Sunday walk in the woods. These stay-at-home dads are onto something, and as for the mums, well they have stitched us up. It's not that bad.

I called Harry hoping to sniff him out for more work only to discover he was back in hospital having treatment. Was he though?

"Not feeling good, son, it's flared up again…" Can cancer flare up? "… I'll be in for a few more days they reckon. I have good news though, we may have a run of gigs in Switzerland."

"OK, Harry, when Switzerland turns into a definite you let me know until then rest up."

"Adam, before you go, I need my commission for the writing work you're doing, now more than ever really."

One of the perks of writing for Glen was he paid on the day and directly into my account. If I was organised I would've immediately transferred fifteen-percent to Harry and then only spent what was mine. But if I was organised I'd have a better agent.

"I'll post you a cheque, Harry. You still use cheques, right?"

"Could you transfer direct into my bank? I may not be home for a while, given my situation."

And what situation was that, Harry? Not being able to look yourself in the mirror?

"Sure, Harry, not a problem."

It was a problem. Highly suspicious diagnosis aside, you know your career is going backwards when you ring your agent and it costs *you* money.

Lucy said she would call as soon as the plane landed but she never did. This morning I began to worry. I checked the news, no plane crash, maybe she got into an accident driving from the airport? It's a horrible feeling, having to plan your new life.

I really drifted away. I put the kids into boarding school and go backpacking through Asia to grieve. After a few months of soul searching I meet a Swedish woman called Helga. Mid-twenties, funny, educated, attracted to middle-aged men with no discernible skills. We open up a bar in Vietnam. Both tall, we decide to call it 'Knee Hi' – which sounds Vietnamese but probably isn't. 'It's our little joke about little people', Helga would say with her potentially racist voice. A year later we rename the bar 'Ho Chi Shin' as it's much funnier. Life is one great big piss-take of short Vietnamese people after another. That is until my nemesis, Hypothetical Greg rocks up and lures Helga away, by inviting her to his weekly skydiving sessions. "The countryside really comes alive at ten thousand feet, you should come with me one time, Helga."

"Yaa, yaa, I'd love to come with you."

Fuck off, Greg. The phone rang right as I was set to tamper with Greg's imaginary parachute.

Lucy was safe she just got caught up in it all. I told her about the kids and how we're all fine and missing her and how Helga ran away with Greg but it's okay because the phone rang and they're not real. Lucy feels betrayed. Mainly by Greg as she really had her eye on him.

"I can win him back," she said.

"Well, you'll have to buy a ticket to figment town."

"I already have. I've been on the Greg train since you first mentioned him. Next stop... Greg. Toot Toot!"

I am eternally grateful to be married to someone who understands me.

I may have underestimated the simplicity of being a single parent. Then again, you have to learn the system before you can game it. I have 'get dressed, put clothes on and get out the door' down pat. Hopefully tomorrow we'll remember the books-and-bag-combo the teachers keep banging on about. The after-school run is the real killer. The zen power move is to get there ten minutes early, park across the street and casually stroll on up to collect your no doubt happy and polite child. You might be so inclined as to listen to some music on your headphones whilst picking flowers from the nearby meadow as you wait. Perhaps you'll see a deer. Why not? You're organised and perfect. What you won't see is us less than perfect parents, who stupidly think it might be okay to try the school carpark. And why shouldn't we? These are our children, we're in a car, this is a carpark, it all makes perfect sense. And it would, if everyone drove a Prius. Unfortunately every second parent thinks it's perfectly reasonable to pick their child up in a Monster Truck. These beasts obscure all vision, you can never see your kid, and if you dare come to a halt for more than twenty-seconds you risk an accident. One poor sod was too slow to load their child's tuba into his car boot and it ended up crushed by a Monster Truck that was late for hockey practice. Luckily for my kids their dad has an Australian accent. They've learnt to hone in on my nasally screams. "Albie! Lizzy!" They hear my call, then dash to the proximity of my voice before jumping blind into our moving car. It gives me confidence knowing that if they're no good academically they can always become stunt doubles.

Today's pick up was a real pressure cooker situation because we had to somehow make it to tennis squad training. What a self-inflicted ball ache. I took my frustrations out on the kids too which never feels good. I yelled at Albie because he accidentally, probably on purpose, lost his spelling sheet out the window and Lizzie kept crying because she wasn't getting invited to any birthday parties. Things only got worse when I forgot the most important thing of all.

"Did you bring snacks, Dad?" Albie asked.

"No, was I supposed to?"

"Nooooo! Worst dad ever," screamed Lizzie.

"I miss Mum," said Albie. I did too.

We got to tennis ten minutes late and Garry Foxe was there, looking super smug knowing he'd played us beautifully. Get them when they're weak and flustered from the school-run. What kind of arsehole makes kids believe they have talent? There must have been ten of them on that court. They can't all be winners.

All this because I didn't want to spend money on a kitchen. Now my next eight Tuesday evenings will be spent standing in the cold drizzle talking to Tennis Dads. I can't compete with these people. It's a rich man's sport. Tennis Dads drive Beamers and wear slippers on Sundays and eat crepes for breakfast. I don't even know what crepes are. I think they're pancakes but I wouldn't bet my Beamer on it, as I don't have one. I can't fit in with the Posh Posse.

━━━━━━━━━━━━━━━━━

With clear skies and little to no tailwind assistance we got the school-run done, from breakfast table to front-gate, in under twenty minutes which I believe is a family PB.

━━━━━━━━━━━━━━━━━

Seventeen minutes and thirty-four seconds! It's the school drop-off version of breaking the four-minute mile. Now that we've cracked eighteen minutes anything is possible.

We've got it down to a fine art.

Albie sleeps in his school shorts while Lizzie lays all her clothes out the night before. I stopped brushing my teeth which is a handy decoy to any odour associated with me wearing yesterday's underpants. Realistically they could be from the day before yesterday, life is blurring into one set of pants. The time I'm saving by no longer whipping old jocks off to hook new ones on is significant. Lucy won't know herself when she adopts my new system. It's just little changes. For example, we've converted to scrambled eggs as they require no toast and less chewing. We're each on a strip of microwaved bacon for protein. Kids' teeth are done before food because why go upstairs twice? I carry their bags; Albie enjoys a jog and Lizzie loves the scooter. Whereas we used to have to get up around six, now I'm more than comfortable sleeping in until half seven. As long as we're out of the house by eight we always scrape through the gates on time.

It started Wednesday after school. Lizzie, apropos of nothing, opened the fridge, put her hand in the crisper and started talking to her new best friend, Marty the Tomato. That's right, my daughter has a pet tomato.

Marty isn't much of a talker, he embarrasses easily and prefers a flat surface. Lizzie's given him his very own sleep sock and keeps him at the foot of the stairs. I insisted that he can't sleep in her room just in case she starts sleep walking again and squashes him.

Our once super-fast morning school run has turned into a dawdle as Lizzie insists on showing Marty every puddle, hedge and tree along the way.

The drop-off mums think a five-year-old girl with a pet tomato is 'adooooorable 'and 'soooo cuuuute' but I'm more inclined to think it's 'a taaaad SpecTrumyyyy'. What can I say? I don't like Marty. He makes me feel like the third wheel. Yesterday after school I tried to snap Lizzie out of it by launching into an abrupt karaoke session which is big for me as I hate all forms of noise. There I was belting out The Nut Bush in the lounge room, giving it some peak Tina Turner, when Lizzie asked me to be quiet because Marty needed his nap. It was like being punched in the face, which really is peak Tina. With Albie glued to the TV and Lizzie befriending salad I actually feel lonely.

I sat by myself last night just looking at Marty and his bulbous red head. Plopped there without a worry in the world, knowing that in the morning he'll get all the love. But who pays the bills, Marty? Who is making sure the uniforms aren't covered in last week's grime? Who is getting up early to make eggs? Who sprays your sleep sock with Febreze?

I miss my wife.

My new favourite saying is, 'New Rule!'

And the new rule is, if Albie mentions Fortnite one more time I will drop him off to school wearing nothing but jazz hands. December is a cold month so it won't go well for either of us but mortifying embarrassment feels like my only remaining option. That or we become fully Amish.

Every two minutes it comes at me in different forms. 'How come? Why not? What if? Maybe I?' Over and over again, the torturous moans of a whiny and disappointed child. His real calling could be interrogating terrorists. After two hours of incessant pestering even the most tight-lipped criminal will spill their guts.

I get it. All the other kids are allowed to play Fortnite. They talk to each other online while playing it. They bond. It's the latest cool fad. Albie feels left out. It's horrible. I understand. But my insides are screaming that this game is violent and highly addictive. He played it once at a friend's house for six hours and then spent the next three days telling me about his one 'kill'. The vibes aren't great.

It feels like an online version of Cowboys and Indians but without the fresh air and exercise. It leaches kids of their dopamine and parents of their money.

Don't worry though, it's free to join but if your kid wants to be accepted socially then you'll need to buy designer Guns and Skins. Guns & Skins? Even the language they use is that of a serial killer. "Purple skins are epic, Dad, but I want orange as that's legendary but they do cost. Maybe for my birthday?" Some prick computer genius has figured out how to turn nagging into an arms race for ten-year-olds! And they'll always want more. What's the next iteration going to be? A game where you pay big to choke out cats! To get to level two you have to mutilate sheep or strangle a sex-worker? Sorry, the murdering of prostitutes is already happening in Grand Theft Auto. Another game some of these parents are letting their ten years old kids play. Ten! "We just can't get little Johnny to read." No shit! You let him stay up late smoking the digital version of crack cocaine. Of course books are going to feel a little dull. And yet, somehow, I'm the bad guy for suggesting my boy wait until he turns twelve before he starts sucking on the digital dopamine pipe.

━━━━━━━━━━━━━━━━━━━━━━━━

Marty caused quite the stir at the supermarket. The looks we got. The other shoppers stared at Lizzie, as if she had stepped out of the pages of a Stephen King novel.

"Is that girl talking to a tomato?"

So, what if she is? We're in a new progressive age.

It only got worse at the checkout. The jobsworth scanning my fruit asked Lizzie if she could weigh her tomato. I gave her a quick rundown of why that wasn't necessary. But like all good jobsworths she didn't believe me.

"Very cute, can I weigh him?" she asked, as if I was deranged.

"No really, it genuinely is her pet tomato, she calls it Marty."

"So do you, Daddy."

"Yes, I do," I said with pride before leaning in and whispering. "But I'd prefer to call him delicious!" Not a zinger but it kept the ball in the air. I was going for a laugh but would've taken a smile. I wasn't expecting her to whisper back, "Let me weigh the tomato or I'll call my manager."

"You honestly think I'm trying to steal a tomato?"

"I do."

"Then call your manager!"

There is no greater feeling than knowing that you're provably right. The joy on my face as I stood my ground, management all around me pointing fingers, people in the queue behind us offering to give me money to end their pain, the chaos, the mayhem and all the time I knew I was infallible. I was so confident about my position I actually started a sentence with, "riddle me this?" and it felt amazing.

"Riddle me this people. Why would I go to all the trouble to train my daughter to befriend a tomato?

What's in it for me? Surely, I'd train her to have a pet bottle of Champagne? I could do with a pet bottle of Champagne. We'd call her Charlotte, a bubbly girl prone to blowing her top. Or maybe my daughter could be best mates with Rib-Eye Robbie? What about Flat Screen Phil? He's always good for a story."

"I'm not following you," said one of the mouth breathing idiots.

"Of course you don't follow me because if you could follow me your job wouldn't involve scanning my cashews."

Lizzie stood by the trolley covering Marty's ears. A shame really because this was some of my best work. Security walked up to the manager and gave him the good news.

"We apologise for the misunderstanding, sir, please allow us to take ten percent off your bill. Jenny, can you sort that?"

"Yes, Jenny, can you sort that? Let me know if you need me to do the maths." I got Lizzie and Marty to wave at the CCTV camera on the way out, it was a *thank you* wave you to the security person who had saved us ten pounds and forty-three pence. It did cross my mind that I could actually train Lizzie to become mates with Champagne. After what happened today, if she walked in with an empty bottle and walked out with a full one, they would have to believe me.

———————————————

Only six days, twelve hours and twenty-two minutes until Lucy comes back home.

———————————————

The Amazon delivery guy knocks too loudly. It's always the same story. I'll be at the 'drool down the chin' stage of my mid-morning nap when what I assume is a SWAT team belts at my door. I come out with my hands up.

"Please don't shoot! Oh, you're the delivery guy. Which means… these must be the underpants I ordered after the last time you nearly broke down my door. And judging by the warm burning sensation that is currently dribbling down my leg I'd say not a moment too soon."

Today's package was a waffle maker.

Months ago Lucy suggested that we buy a waffle maker because she believed the waffles from the shops were full of sugar. I suggested that a much cheaper solution would be for our kids to not eat waffles. Toast would suffice. But nothing says you've lost a waffle maker argument more than sitting alone in a kitchen staring at a new waffle maker. Lucy is really playing the 'I'm burying my dad' card to bring useless shit into the house.

———————————————

Spoke to Lucy on the phone. Mentioned the waffle maker. Regret it.

I don't know why being called a tight arse is derogatory. Isn't a tight ass what people want? The other option is less than ideal.

"How is he with his finances? He has a really loose and flabby ass. No sphincter control whatsoever. It's kind of gross."

Funeral went well.

———————————————

Graham came around with a pie.

"We heard Lucy's dad passed and Jess mentioned she was back in Oz, and you were on your own with the kids, so we thought you might want a night off cooking."

"Thanks, Graham, you shouldn't have. An actual pie! At my house…" Essentially from a stranger, we've had *maybe* four chats in five years, three about rain, one where he shouted from his front-door that we were neighbours and his name was Graham. "…What a lovely gesture…"

"Well, we have to look out for one another… don't we? What are the lyrics to that song your lot sing?

Neighbours should be there for one another, that's when good neighbours become good friends," Graham sang that last bit. It was like being serenaded by two quarrelling cats.

"I was more a Home and Away guy myself. Graham, I'm so sorry but the kids are in the bath. Thanks for the pie though. Lucy's back soon so we should…" I didn't want to say, 'catch up' because that would involve, well, catching up.

"No pressure, Adam, as Jess says to me, 'you do you'. Enjoy the pie."

Graham's probably the happiest man on the street. The plumber who goes out and plumbs all day but still finds time to make sure the neighbours are fed. What a guy! Everyone loves Graham. He's always good for a wave and shouting your name from across the street in his thick Welsh accent. Everyone just absolutely loves Graham. Great Guy! Love him. Love! Love! Love! Graham! Graham! Graham!

How do I turn a guy who drops off pies into an arsehole? It's not healthy. Do I have to bake him a pie now? Is that how this works? What is pie etiquette? Can I leave the empty dish on his doorstep? Or do I knock and have a conversation about how good the pie was? It was delicious. The kids and I loved it! Our first home cooked meal in a week.

In the end, I wrote, 'thanks for the pie' onto a post-it note, stuck it on the empty dish and left it on Graham's doorstep. That way he gets his dish back, we show we're grateful and I don't have to speak to him for another two years. Perfect.

There's such a big difference between the person I want to be compared to the person I am.

He said it, so I did it.

It was always going to be a risk. But you have to follow through. You must. Otherwise, kids take the piss. Plus trauma can be good for a child. Woody Harrelson's dad was a hitman and look at him now, he's a famous movie star and one of my go to party facts. It's not as if I didn't warn Albie. He was warned. He should not have been surprised when I hopped in the car wearing nothing but a trench coat. He was told in no uncertain terms to shut up about Fortnite yet he refused to heed to the threat. Well, after this morning's events the heed is on. The poor kid, having to endure the fear that his naked-underneath dad would get out of the car, shed his coat and sing New York, New York. He will never not heed again.

Albie was beside himself, screaming, 'Dad, please don't do it. Please!' Tears streamed down his face. He was shaking. I immediately knew I'd pushed him too far but there was no out clause as I hadn't packed pants. I couldn't pull over and pop on a set of consoling clothes. I was irreversibly naked and we were mid drop off. Bumper to bumper of solid aggressive traffic. I had no choice but to keep driving. As I had no real plans of getting out of the car I thought I may as well go with it.

"My little town blues, I'm melting away." With each lyric I sang louder and louder.

"If I can make it there…"

"Dad, please! Don't do it. Please!"

"I can make it… anywhere." Lizzie was waving her hands in the air. Marty rolling around in the middle seat. Albie was distraught.

"Dad, please!"

"These Vagabond shoes…"

It was like this for three full versus right to the front of his school.

"New Yorrrrkkkkk!"

"Please, Dad, I'll never mention Fortnite again, ever, never ever, please don't get out of the car!"

"The next time you mention that game, there will be no coat. Do you understand me?"

"Yes, Dad, I promise I won't ever mention it again."

"All right then. Off you go."

He opened the door and ran away, scared shitless. Lizzie trailed behind in a daze, unable to grasp what had just happened. She offered a wave but in a 'please get help from a therapist' kind of way. Albie didn't look back. He always looked back. I wondered if I'd lost him forever. Then in a moment of complete dumb-fuckery I drove into the car in front of me.

It's a myth that the truth sets you free, especially if you have to answer the question 'why are you naked in a trench coat outside a school?'

Claire Drysdale, best described as systemically rich, hopped out of her high-end Beamer and panic-walked towards the rear of her car.

"I've got children in the back seat."

"I'm so sorry, completely my fault. Are they OK?" I yelled from the top inch of my window.

"They're very shaken. Well? Come and give me your number," she said already taking photos of the damage.

"I cannot do that."

"Why?"

"Err, umm, because I'm paralysed from the waist down. Come to the window and we can swap details," said the man who was fresh out of ideas.

Being naked on a school run is one thing but pretending to be disabled was a new low, even for me, yet it did force her hand. She had no choice but to walk up to my window. Cars honked their horns and a crowd of students watched on from the playground.

"I'm so sorry…"

"What's your number?"

"067 4577 0391."

"Right, here's my card." She handed me her card. Her name was Claire Drysdale and she was a solicitor at Drysdale & Drysdale. Brilliant, I'd just rammed a lawyer. Fantastic. Love that. Love. Love. Love. That! That! That!

"Hang on. Are you not wearing trousers? You're not wearing trousers! Are you a pervert? I'm calling the police!"

"No no! I'm doing the drop off. My kids literally just ran into the school." I yelled for Lizzie but she was nowhere to be seen, so I whipped out my phone which was uncomfortably near my crotch.

"Look at my phone, here is a picture of me and my wife and our two children. See here's Elizabeth, my daughter, with her brother. We're the Vincents. Ring the school if you like. Please, I've had a shit of a morning. It's raining. Their mother is away burying her dad. I'm barely hanging on."

"You're standing in this photo, recently paralysed then?"

"OK, that was a lie, I panicked. The truth is I told my son if he didn't stop talking about Fortnite I'd drop him off to school naked. This is me following through. As a parent you have to appreciate 'the follow-through'. If you say you're going to do it…"

"You've got to follow-through… Right, so you're not a pervert but you are a psycho?" she said as the cars behind us honked their horns in anger. Claire didn't register the building tension or see the need to move which I think makes her the psycho.

"I'm not a psycho! I was simply making a point."

"Doesn't look that simple to me, it looks very confusing. And as far as Fortnite goes, it's harmless. My children play it and they're fine. You've just dropped your children off to school naked. What do you think does more damage? You'll be hearing from me, Mr Vincent." And with that Claire Drysdale strutted back to her car.

"New York!" I yelled from behind the wheel. Full jazz hands. Always follow through.

Danger! Danger! Danger! This is bad, this is very very bad.

Lucy ambushed me on a Zoom call. Judy is flying back with her. Bad! Very, very bad! This is a nightmare situation. A Judy visit is the equivalent of a baboon ripping off your bottom jaw and having to spend the rest of your life trying to chew grapes. I'm angry, I'm scared and I feel used.

"She needs us, she feels lost," said Lucy still wearing black.

"Lost? Couldn't she move in with your brother? She loves Miles!"

"We all love Miles but he's an idiot." This is true, Miles is an idiot. He lost all of his money shipping mobile phone cases over from China. He spent months telling us the shipment was on its way and it was, unfortunately for Miles though, it was a shipment of old, and very much obsolete, Nokia cases. The man is professionally stupid.

"Could she not take a cruise for six months? Figure out what she wants." This was me buying time but it was no use, Lucy's response was to hold up the plane tickets and then hang up. I got a text saying, "Sorry, my phone died. We get into Heathrow on Sunday at eleven p.m. Don't be angry x."

Don't be angry? Of course I'm angry. One of the few perks of leaving Australia was not having to be judged by this person at close range. Now I'm set to be placed right in front of the cannon.

Do I not get a say? Surely I have a say? This isn't a waffle maker this is my mother-in-law and if she prolongs her stay, my life is over. My sex life! I'll never get an erection again knowing she's there, plotting my downfall. The woman who tried to set her daughter up with the prat, Tim Sullivan, on our wedding day.

"He's a qualified surgeon now, has his own practice. You guys should have lunch."

"Jesus, Judy! We're about to cut the cake."

Fuckety fuckety fuck. I cannot overstate how this will affect my life.

Pros: The kids adore her. She likes to clean.

Cons: I'll be figuratively fist fucked in the arse by this woman's very shadow on a daily basis for the rest of my miserable shitting life.

Other than that, everything will be fine. Fine! I will simply have to learn to love Judy! Love! Love! Love! Judy! Judy! Judy!

And one day I might actually believe it. Who am I kidding?

First Judy, now this! Marty is missing! Lizzie's mortified. Aren't we all? She blames Albie. Albie blames her. It's a nightmare. We spent the morning searching the house. We moved the couch, I think I did my back checking behind her bed. All the time knowing that last night, I put Marty into a BLT. I was hungry. Guilty. Not only was my punishment having to listen to the kids squabble, then pretending to care for Marty's whereabouts but now I'm in the ridiculous situation where I have to go to the supermarket and buy a similar looking tomato. Me, in the fruit & veg section, holding up my phone looking at old photos hoping to find a match for Marty 2.0. It doesn't help that he was starting to look shabby. I'm going to have to age the new Marty in the microwave.

It only took Judy thirty-seconds. That was a new record. I vacuumed the entire house, scrubbed the floors, I did all the laundry, made every bed and decluttered every surface. The house hadn't looked this good since I tried to save the kitchen and completely misrepresented the shambles we'd been living in while Lucy was away. Yet, Judy, gets two feet inside the home, sneezes and asks me when I last dusted. It was almost impressive. She must've rehearsed. I imagine her in the toilet on the plane, "Achew! No I need to hit the 'a' harder and elongate the 'cheeew' *aaa*cheeew. Better. That'll get under his skin." And then she walked back to her seat with a maniacal laugh.

It must have been a rough flight. Normally Judy will hit me with a barrage of thinly veiled digs about my long-term earning potential. Tim Sullivan usually always gets a mention.

"Did I tell you Tim's just bought a new house? Yes, he's moved to the Sunshine Coast, very posh." But tonight it was just the sneeze and then she grabbed her luggage and hauled herself to bed. Lucy collapsed on the couch and then gave me the bad news. Her mum really did have nowhere to go.

"She's got no one, Adam, her house is gone, she just needs a few months with us. You know Dad left her nothing."

"Bankruptcy will do that. Can't Miles help?"

"He's done as much as he can but he's still on meds and just can't handle it."

"We could always move back to Melbourne?"

"No, I can't have that chat again, the kids are settled. She just needs a few months."

"Months! She doesn't know anyone here, she'll get lonely. At her age, three months is really ten years."

"She knows us and Mum is such a go-getter, she'll make new friends."

"What about all her old friends?"

"They're all dead or dying or boring. She's ready for a change."

"A change? She's sixty-eight, her next change is reincarnation."

"Look, you may not like it but she's staying with us. End of…"

And with that Lucy smiled, kissed me on the head and walked upstairs to a spotless bedroom that went for nothing, because she was too exhausted to care.

Lucy woke me up at four-thirty a.m. bored from jet lag.

"Look who's using the waffle maker!" I then had a chocolate waffle stuffed into my mouth and a very flirtatious eyebrow was raised. I felt a stirring in my loins… and then the kids ran into the room and jumped on the bed.

"Mummy!"

"Dad dropped me off to school naked."

"What?"

"I'll explain later on."

Judy waltzed in wearing a tracksuit and a headband.

"GG!" The kids screamed. GG is short for *Greatest Granny* which is very debatable.

"My darlings!" The kids rushed her and she wrapped them up in her sinewy arms.

"Oh I missed you guys. Morning, Adam... slept in again I see." It was quarter to five in the morning. Was it a joke? Was it serious? This is what Judy does. She gets in your head and she stays there until you replace her with a gun.

I am flummoxed. I am discombobulated. I am angry. I am a therapist's holiday house.

Sat in a Tesco car park and cried.

Judy's morning call starts on the dot of six with the lifting and the heaving of kettle bells. They were my kettle bells but she noticed they were covered in dust and asked if she could put them to good use. Judy loves jibes. It kills me that a sixty-eight-year-old lady is upstairs doing my squats. I hear her groaning as she lunges away asking the universe for more time. The kettle bells crash onto the wooden floorboards above, it's Judy's way of letting us all know she's completed another set. Forty-five minutes, every morning for the last three weeks! I sit up in bed and watch the light fittings shake while pieces of ceiling land in my first cup of tea.

"Who lifts weights at sixty-eight? She should be packing her bags."

"Have you met my mum? She's not dying any time soon."

"Soon? I'd be happy with 'maybe later' or 'sometime down the track'. She has the half-life of plutonium."

"This conversation is getting old, Adam."

"I know and your mum is getting younger."

───────────────

Got a text from Claire Drysdale.

'Claire Drysdale here, you crashed into my car whilst naked near a school, the repair quote came in at £1700. Going through insurance? Or cash? Please respond by the end of the day.'

Who has seventeen hundred pounds to throw at someone else's car repair? Lawyers! They have no idea how real people live.

'Hi, Claire, I wasn't naked I was wearing a trench

coat because I wanted to traumatise my son into not ever mentioning the game Fortnite, which despite what you think is a highly addictive and dangerous game. I will be going through insurance.'

These people…

━━━━━━━━━━━━━━━━━━━━━━━━━

Graham brought around another pie. Can you believe this prick? He knocked on the door after work.

"Hi Adam, I just thought I'd drop in a 'welcome to Bedford' pie for Judy."

"Oh thanks, Graham, you shouldn't have…" How many times do I have to say this before he gets the point? "…She's out shopping with Lucy and the kids… and… how did you meet Judy?"

"Oh I'm forever bumping into Judy on my early morning walk. She'll be going left and I'll be going right but we both stop in the middle and have our regular natter. I think it's fantastic that she's moving in. The street could do with some of her get up and go."

"It sure is nice having her stay… sorry Graham… What do you mean moving in?"

"That's what she told me."

"Moving in? That's the first I've heard of it but I'm never privy to the big decisions. Wow, just moving in and completely ruining my sense of everything. That is a game changer. What horrific information! Thanks again for the pie, it had better be good because this is hard news to swallow." And with that I shot off up the street like a crazed madman holding a pie.

"Very well, Adam, you do you, oh and congratulations on your infomercials by the way. I can't stay up late enough to watch them as I'm asleep by nine on most nights, but I hear they're brilliant," yelled Graham as I made my way around the corner.

How did Graham know about Judy moving in before me? First, he drops off pies, now he's dropping off family secrets! Judy was meant to be a two-month blip, a fast tracked tour-de-merde, a gnawing ice cream headache that only dissipates once her plane takes off. But for her to move in! Announcing herself every day with grunts and groans, judging my every move, scoffing at my inept parenting style, chiding my complete lack of work ethic, rolling her eyes whenever I forget to take out the bins or open up the new cheese before finishing the old cheese. No! I cannot have that. And Graham knowing before me, well that does take the Stilton.

Unconscionable! Excessive! Unwarranted! These will be a few of the words I bandy about in what now feels like a rather winnable argument. It's not often I get one of those. I've started many a verbal stoush fully aware I was in the wrong but this here is a moral high ground situation which feels like uncharted territory. An argument that's winnable! What a concept! The power it gives you. I see how this goes down. Lucy and I will be standing in the kitchen. I'll yell, 'The fucking neighbours knew! Graham knew! Graham? The guy who bakes pies because he's got no friends, he knew before your own husband! Why that's… unconscionable!' Then I raise my eyebrows, throw a tea towel on the floor and walk away fuming. Lucy, seeing the error of her ways, will chase me across the house before apologising profusely. She'll try the 'I don't know what came over me 'angle. I'll ignore it. Maybe she will play the dead dad card but that will go for nothing. He is after all, dead. I won't say the words 'move on sweetheart' but they'll be written on my face. Yep, the way I see it, our little skirmish ends with Lucy making us a cup of tea and me graciously accepting her apology while putting her waffle maker up for sale on eBay. We'll agree that any notion of a mother-in-law moving in is all a bit much and while on the subject of stupid decisions, we should cancel the new kitchen, as life is too short for such extravagant frivolities. Meanwhile Judy, having seen the pain she's caused, will be upstairs packing her bags readying herself for the flight back to Australia. End scene.

Feels rock solid.

I'll keep the winnable argument close to my chest. Lucy can have a couple of days to confess her sins and who knows, maybe Graham got his wires crossed. It's possible, the guy is a plumber who bakes pies, he's got a screw loose somewhere. If I've heard nothing by Friday, I will be properly chucking a tea towel.

———————————————

Thursday T minus forty hours until winnable argument commences.

Mood: Certain.

Financial Life expectancy: Fifty-seven and a half but with the winnable argument this could easily bounce back up to the low sixties.

———————————————

The problem with taking Albie to tennis practice is that he's called Albie. I want to believe he's got talent, but really?

I sat there and watched him hit the ball for an hour with the other nuffs. I didn't see any skill from anyone. At least half the time he hit the ball into the net. If you can't beat the object that never moves, then I struggle to see how you're a tennis protégé. They're aiming for the gap between the clouds and the top of the tape yet none of these kids could make it work. But on the rare occasions when Albie would hit a winner, Garry, the con artist coach, really turned it on. He would look at the other coaches with raised eyebrows, as if he had just discovered Britain's next Wimbledon champ. It was embarrassing. I warned Lucy that this would happen. Garry is no different to all day care centres and birthday magicians that have tried the same trick. They all hear the name 'Albie' then think, 'Albert' which leads to thoughts of money.

Everyone knows Albert is a posh boy's name. It's right up there with Rupert and Bartholomew. The name isn't quite a Marmaduke but it could have dinner with one. It's aristocratic. I told Lucy when he was born, "If we call him, Albert, we'll have to be prepared for people to take the piss." She, of course, thought I was being paranoid and ridiculous insisting that Albert means 'noble' and that the world needs more noble men. What rubbish! If the name 'Albert' translates into anything it's 'Expensive'. Garry is just another rip-off merchant in a long line of rip-off merchants who are intent on proving me right. He doesn't see talent, he sees yacht parties with high-end Champagne, and quail eggs on rye for lunch at the polo club. He sees money! But he is very much mistaken. Which is what I told him when he pulled me to one side and suggested Albie would benefit from some 'one-to-one lessons'. The look on the poor man's face.

"I have to tell you, Albie has got all the makings of a neat little player. He just needs to work on his tech…"

"Let me stop you there, Garry. I know you mean well and we all have to make a living but you're barking up the wrong money tree. OK?"

"I'm sorry?"

"How do I put this? We don't really work to an Albert budget. You hear 'Albert' when really he's more

84

of a… 'Kyle.'"

"I'm not following you."

"Sure, you're not. Look, I thought I'd be earning Albert cash. I really did. But my agent got cancer and even though that's questionable, life hasn't gone as planned. I'm optimistic that maybe one day we'll be back on Dave money. Dave money feels doable, heck I'd settle for some 'Kevin coin' but 'the big Albert bucks' are not going to happen. Okay? I mean if I was on Albert money, I wouldn't be living in a semi-detached house in Bedford would I?"

"I honestly don't know what it is you're talking about I just think he's got potential, Adam. I'm happy to give him a couple of free lessons if that helps."

"The long con, brilliant. Look, the truth is, he's only here because I didn't want to fork out for a new kitchen and that backfired. Do you know how many tennis lessons you get from a quartz worktop?"

"No idea."

"Loads. There's a potential Andy Murray being built at my house next month…"

"I have a lesson to get to. Look it'd be great to see Albie at squad training."

"I bet it would."

And after that poor Garry trudged off knowing the truth. To borrow a tennis term, advantage me.

The challenge was who could yell the loudest without being heard by either Judy or the children. I'm not saying it went badly but at one point I brought up a recently purchased waffle maker that had only been used once. Lucy saw that waffle maker and raised it with a vibrator that has *never* been used and suggested I go fuck myself. I folded. And today's entry is coming live from the couch. It was meant to be a winnable argument!

I opened strong.

"Graham knew about your mum moving in before I did!"

"I told you she was moving in!" Did she though?

"No, you said your mum was staying for a few months." As the words left my mouth I realised how naive I was in believing this. She had the dual passport, of course Lucy would ask her to use it.

"Well, her stay has been extended, indefinitely," Lucy blurted this out like it wasn't up for debate. Ha!

"So I don't get a say?" I had my shoulders shrugged and mouth open letting the other party know that their previous statement was in fact, stupid.

"Yes, of course you 'get a say' but it has to be 'yes'." Lucy mimicked my shrugged shoulders and slack jaw but added a hefty dose of sarcasm around 'get a say 'which breaks several rules of the Geneva convention.

"Well, if I do 'get a say', that say is a big fat 'noooo!'" I doubled down on the shrugged shoulders open mouthed combo, matched her on the sarcasm but also threw in some swirling of the hips around the 'nooo'.

"So you're kicking a sixty-eight year old woman out of her home? My mother, out of my home?" Lucy followed this statement up with a still-face stare down. This is where it gets real. When used properly the still-face stare down is lethal. I once saw a guy self-combust after a still faced stare down. It's what we call in the biz, 'scary'.

I had to use all my tricks... "Don't play the 'old ' card on me, your mum can bench press more than I can," ...self-deprecating humour that was factually correct but also emphasised my point.

"Miles said he'll chip in with her living expenses. Plus she's a built in babysitter and the kids love her." Aha! I was winning! She was changing tact by bringing up her loser brother. The guy that once borrowed fifty dollars for rent money and came back with a cheesecake. It was a good cheesecake, fruit on top, we all had a slice, but what a loser.

"Miles is a dappy fool! He'll never chip in and you know it. But the much bigger point is I never get a say, in anything, where we live, how we eat, what we do..." Damn it! Her change of tact worked. I was now talking rubbish.

"With Mum here as a babysitter I can ask for more hours at work."

"What? Really?"

"They've been wanting me to do more hours and so have our finances."

"We don't need the money if you don't want to do the work. I can get us through," I said knowing that I couldn't.

"Honey, last week you wrote jokes for a late night infomercial selling water proof pants! We could use the money."

"That was a very big campaign. Pop's Water Proof Pants… the Las Vegas of Pants. What happens in Pop's Pants, stays in Pop's Pants."

"You're a genius."

"Is this the new normal? Taking the piss out of the guy who works two jobs to pay the bills?"

"Two jobs?"

"Writing and I have a gig in Poole next week."

"Paid?"

"Yes, it is a paid gig so ease up on the taking of the piss."

"I thought Pop's Pants could take the piss?"

"That was good."

"I try."

"Oh, you're trying all right."

"Look, I just think we could make the most of Mum being here to help out. I think it's wonderful you're making a living from doing what you love, but we're almost broke."

"We're not almost broke!"

"You hit a *BMW*! The insurance people rang me

yesterday. Our premiums are going to go up by hundreds. Mum stays."

Oh Jesus! She had this up her sleeve the entire time. Winnable argument my arse! It was a trap!

"Yes, I had a slight altercation on the school run." Fucking Drysdale and Drysdale!

"Was this when you were naked?"

"I was wearing a trench coat! It was raining and don't talk to me about money. You haven't made waffles in weeks."

And we know what happens next. I go fuck myself.

━━━━━━━━━━━━━━━━━

I woke up this morning in the lounge room only to see Judy eating porridge in the dark.

"Morning, Judy."

"Morning, Adam."

"You sleep well?"

"Good. How was your night?"

"Great."

And with that we both knew. This was how it would be until one of us died.

━━━━━━━━━━━━━━━━━

I'm halfway through a month long writing contract with

Glen. Every day, he's hocking a different product. From water bottles that heat up your soup, to rowing machines that fix your spine, to mega memory pillows that increase your IQ. I'm not saying the products are dodgy but that's only because Glen is paying me twelve hundred pounds a week to help promote them. I can't lie, it's a brilliant job. I get paid to write gags about pillows. But working in London is a different beast, especially when you're an outsider. There's an emotional toll that you're expected to pay whenever crossing over the M25 into the realm of the special people. The constant jibes that you'll never be as hip as a fully paid-up Londoner. Every chance they get. Even Glen, my Australian ally was getting in on it.

"Britain's a fuck'n shit-hole but if you're gonna up sticks and move here you may as well live in the fuck'n most exciting turd. But Bedford, fuck'n I can't work out if you're a dumb cunt or a fuck'n poor cunt," said Glen the most Australian Australian to have ever graced the streets of London.

"Probably both skipper, feel free to pay me more. Hahaha." One thing I've learnt about being a writer. The talent has to win. Glen gets to call me 'cunt' but I can only call him 'skipper' and even that is mood dependent. Not that Glen is the problem. He's a harmless halfwit. It's the producer, Francis. Next level prick. I don't know exactly what it is about young, happy, affluent, childless Londoners that irks me but it may have something to do with them being young, happy, affluent, childless Londoners.

Francis is the good looking buck with a large Adam's apple and droopy eyes, who constantly chews gum to keep the generator for his brain working. The minute his jaw relaxes the power stops and his head plops forward. That is until his teeth re-enter gnash mode and his noggin pops back up. Like most twenty something's in London he's probably a moron but could be a genius. I don't know what a producer does but I'm pretty sure one of his tasks is to make me feel old and tired. For the last three Monday's he's started every meeting with a story about how his life is better than mine.

"I had the best weekend, Adam, it was amazing."

"I'm sure it was, Francis." Why don't you spend the next twenty minutes rubbing my nose in it.

"We started off in Soho where dinner was this wild crazy virtual food hunt. It's amazing. You have to go. Trust me, you haven't lived. They don't give you a menu they give you a VR headset! Before you know it you're walking around in a forest holding a cross bow, stalking your meal. I shit you not."

"Please don't!"

"You'll be prowling along the virtual tundra when suddenly in the distance you'll see an elk or a deer, or a bull and when the time is right you aim at whatever you feel like eating, you gently pull the trigger and boom! Twenty minutes later an elk steak appears on your table."

"That does sound amazing!"

"Oh, Adam, don't get me started… After dinner we went to Tomahawks. Have you been to Tomahawks? You haven't lived. They put you in a booth, serve you cocktails and let you throw an axe at a wall. Seriously, it's like darts but with an axe."

"Really?"

"Yeah and it doesn't end there… after Tomahawks we got a call from Messa…" That's the other thing Francis does, he introduces characters and expects me to know who they are.

"…Messa's at Donkey Kong. Adam, have you been to Donkey Kong? Oh…"

"Let me guess, I haven't lived…"

"You haven't lived. You start on the bottom floor, you have to work your way up to the top floor, but here's where it gets tricky… people dress up in monkey suits and throw vodka at you!"

"What?"

"Yeah! I nearly made it to the top level too but I passed out and woke up in the London Eye. I went and had breakfast in Soho then Jess called we dropped some pingers and then her friend Savanah came around and we had a three way."

"Just like that."

"Totally like that. Then we…"

I sit there and listen to Francis regale about his weekend adventures and I don't want him to stop because if he does, it means he's about to ask me that same god-awful question.

"...So how was your weekend?"

Oh, for the love of Christ! Don't ask a man in his forties this question, especially if he doesn't live in *London*. We have no exciting answers. I can't match Francis's youthful exuberance, his beautiful not knowingness, his energetic dumb-fuckery.

"How was my weekend, Francis? I took my kids to the park. Have you been to the park, Francis? You haven't lived. It's full of grass and desperation. Lizzie wanted to go on the seesaw but Albie wanted to go on the climbing frame. So, I pushed Lizzie up and down with my hands for what seemed like an eternity, ironically, I wanted to throw an axe against a wall. Ha! Then Albie wanted me to watch him jump from one rubber tyre to another, for twenty fucking minutes, Francis. Twenty. Cold. Windswept. Minutes! Luckily Lizzie needed to pee, so we rushed off to find a toilet. Unfortunately, you needed forty pence to get into the toilet and I didn't have forty pence on me so I had to take her behind a bush and pull down her pants and hope that everybody nearby realised she was actually my daughter. This is where it gets weird, Francis. I think Lizzie has a wonky vagina because her piss came out at an angle and went straight into my socks. Have you had kids piss in your socks, Francis? You haven't lived. Now, it's around this time that I realised that I can't find Albie. So, I had to pick up my still pissing daughter while frantically calling out for my missing son "Albie!

93

Where are you? Albie!" In my excitement and fear I inadvertently turned Lizzie into a pump action piss pistol. I shot an old lady in the trousers, Francis, with my daughter's vagina, have you ever done that? Shot an old lady in the trousers with your daughter's vagina? It caused quite the commotion which thankfully got Albie's attention as he came running to protect me from an oncoming Zimmer frame. We had to make a hasty exit, so I put Lizzie on my shoulder, Albie by my side and walked their crying and pissing selves home. I washed them off, I cleaned them up, then I let Lizzie watch The Little Mermaid for the hundredth time, Albie lost his noggin playing Among Us and then what did I do? Oh that's right, I cried whilst having a poo! Have you ever done that, Francis? Wiped your arse with toilet paper that has been saturated from your own tears... well you haven't lived."

Francis and I have been dancing this same dance for three weeks now. He makes me feel old and I scare him senseless that one day soon, he'll be me. The sadder my life is the harder he seems to party which only makes me sadder which then makes him party harder. We're stuck in an infinity loop of depression and fear. It causes no end of heart ache and it must be costing Francis a fortune. Vodka based Donkey Kong doesn't sound cheap.

Gig in Poole. Four hour drive there, to do a thirty-minute set and luckily the adrenalin of doing new Pet Tomato material got me through the three hour drive home. Knackered. Came in at half two busting for a piss but no free car spaces nearby. It was Graham's side-gate or my strides. In the end they both got a wash. My steamy piss cloud set-off his night light and I had to scamper down the road drizzling all over myself.

I do wonder if these trips are worth it?

An eight hour round trip for a hundred and seventy pounds that arrives six weeks from now and will probably bounce when I try and cash it. Then you have to minus the forty-five pounds I spent on petrol, the nine pounds and fifty pence I handed over for my sandwich, Mars bar and water combo, the twelve pounds of wear and tear on the car itself plus the fact that my neck is now unable to rotate left so I'm probably looking at three sessions with the physio at thirty-three pounds per session which brings the gig to a net profit of negative seven pounds and forty pence. Comedy! Comedy! Comedy! Love! Love! Love!

Financial life expectancy: fifty-six and three-quarters unless I forgo the physio which might give me another month.

I saw Judy in her underpants. The woman's got pins. Lucy got her extra hours, which means more money, she may have saved us.

———————————————

Garry got in touch with Lucy and convinced her that Albie can play tennis. She's enrolled him for another six weeks' worth of squads and a weekly tennis lesson! Weekly! That's a hundred and twenty pounds a month on tennis. It's almost as if Garry heard through Bedford's very close and tight knit community that Lucy got more hours. That Garry Foxe is a shark.

———————————————

I got the text that every dad dreads but doesn't want to miss out on.

"Adam, are you up for a dad's night out?"

I didn't recognise the number but they knew my name and I was a dad so technically I qualified. I replied with the thumbs up emoji but there was no thumbs up about it, I had agreed to meet a group of dads, most of whom I have met maybe once at a school performance.

I would have nodded and said, "Hey" while shuffling to find my chair. They'd have nodded and said, "Hey" while shuffling to find theirs and then we'd sit down and look for our respective children who would've been dressed as donkeys. That was the extent of my relationship with these men. To go from enduring a nativity play in silence to drinking beer in a pub is a *huge* jump. It's Evil Knievel into the wind. A blind date with dads. Are they crazy?

I mean I want to make the leap. I have no friends. I'm a forty-two-year-old man with no actual mates in a strange land. If the shit goes down, I have no one to turn to. My butcher calls me Skippy, Francis tells me about his three-ways, Glen endearingly calls me a cunt and Graham bakes me pies. These are not the kind of people who will help me in a crises. 'Oh, Adam, why have you got a gun in your mouth? You should call a friend. I'll see if Graham wants to pop over.' That would only help me pull the trigger. What do friends even do? It's been so long. Table tennis? See a band? Talk shit while playing snooker? The very idea of a Dad's Night... it doesn't fill the mind with wild ideas. It sounds like I've picked up the old man from the nursing home and 'I'll have him back by four.'

It's easy for the mums. They all know each other, they chat at the pickups and the drop offs, they have WhatsApp groups that cover everything from lost jumpers to the latest trends in gin. They go to Book Club on Mondays. When they have a mum's night out, they've got hours of water under the bridge. They're practically sisters. On the off chance that they don't have anything to talk about they can always find common ground by chatting about their dickhead husbands. 'Frank's an arsehole' 'So is my Kevin, shall we buy a bottle of prosecco or three and laugh at them?' And they're off, having a good time.

What am I going to do? This is bad. I'm no good with people, I hate most of them but now I've emoji'd myself onto a table full of strangers. Will any of us want to be there? The only thing we have in common is we shagged our wives at roughly the same time. How did the other dads get my number?

Oh God, what if Lucy asked one of the mums to get her husband to include me on the next Dad's Night?

"He doesn't really know anyone and he cries on the toilet."

It's high school all over again. This is a disaster.

━━━━━━━━━━━━━━━━━━━━━━━

Confronted Lucy about the Dad's Night. She denies all involvement, claims she had no idea they were even a thing and is adamant I go as she wants a night in with her mum. So, it's safe to say that tomorrow night was all organised by her.

━━━━━━━━━━━━━━━━━━━━━━━

Mood: Beer fear.

Last night will go down in history as one of the most awkward beginnings to a night out I have ever experienced and I once left the house seeing my parents playing naked twister with the neighbours. I have a visual on the phrase 'Left nipple blue' and I still wasn't prepared for two hours of dry mouth that started last night's shenanigans.

I arrived fifteen minutes late wearing the safe bet combo of jeans, shirt and jumper. Smart, casual, might be a stock broker, could an accountant, but definitely not a jobbing comedian with no future. Always start with vanilla on the first date. You can't rock up in a hyper colour T-shirt and golf pants. That guy smokes crack and only comes out on special occasions.

"Hi everyone, I'm Adam, the new dad in the WhatsApp group," I said with a beaming smile, that was possibly too keen but I wanted to open strong. "Hi Adam," they all murmured and we shook hands and swapped names. Three words here, two there, the odd grunt and then nothing, zip. A silence engulfed the table. I had to check my phone to make sure it wasn't Armistice Day. Was the Foresters Arms a pub for Quakers?

Half a pint in and I wanted out. This bunch had no zing. But I was sure, the universal rule had to be, you can't leave a Dad's Night until the clock strikes ten. However, every minute after ten is a bonus minute and will allow leeway for an earlier exit for future nights out but to up stumps and vamoose before nine at your first outing is beyond the pale. I had to ignore the complete lack of banter and push through. Didn't help that we all looked the same, all between five foot ten and six foot two, no flair in the outfits, no top hats, no mohawks, no pimp coats, just a homogenised clump of slouchy dad meat. Had there been a flat tyre nearby, or an unlit barbecue, perhaps a pram with a wonky wheel, then I'm certain we would have merged into a giant Super Dad and fixed the problem. What we couldn't fix was our complete inability to communicate.

"Which class is your kid in?" I said, hoping to get the ball rolling.

"Mrs Hobb's."

"That's right, I saw you at the Nativity play."

"Yeah."

This glorious interaction was followed by three more minutes of silence. Three minutes! Time it. It's harrowing. I thought I might follow it up with a funny home truth because it was now half passed eight and something had to give.

"I think our wives organised this because they're scared that one of us is going to kill ourselves."

They looked at me like I'd pissed in their beer then hit me with two more minutes of silence. It was like scraping my teeth down a black board. I moved to the question you ask when you've got nothing.

"So, how's work?" What a barnacle on the soul of a man that question is. There are so many better conversation starters. Like:

"Who would win in a fight between an alligator and a gorilla?" Or…

"Both of your kids are hanging from a cliff, you can only save one but they'll never call you Dad again, who do you pick?" Maybe…

"Want to steal a van and see how far we can go before someone cares? I reckon we'd get to Mongolia."

But I lacked the courage.

"Work has its moments."

"Right."

In a normal world people would elaborate on what some of those moments might be but this wasn't normal, it was like talking to bricks. I had no choice but to use the night's safety word.

"Beers?"

I licked my wounds at the bar and went in for round two, beer two.

"Tell me about yourself, mate, what do you do?"

"I sell surgical equipment to hospitals," said some bloke who I think was called John. He was the maverick who wore the light blue sweater.

"Oh great, so you must travel a lot?"

"Yep."

Another minute of actual silence. I checked my shoes to make sure I hadn't stepped in shit.

"Good chat," I actually said that. I said, 'good chat ' in a sarky way because this was going nowhere. I had to let them know that I needed more. But I didn't get more. Instead, I sat amongst a group of men staring at their beers wondering when it would end. Did any of them want to be there? Were they under duress? Had their wives forced them to come because the Australian dad was a bit down and needed cheering up? I couldn't have been the only one. The pain we all must have been experiencing, the abject loneliness. Clearly, we agreed to be there, clearly we wanted to talk about something! At one time in our lives, we all must have danced on tables and rolled down hills and screamed at the stars, we must have vented our dreams and recited poetry, got into fist fights, tongue kissed a stranger in an alley, but here we were sitting in an old British pub with fake antlers on the walls staring into half-drunk lagers waiting for what? What had become of us? None of us had been to war, we had no PTSD to speak of. What happened to the great art of getting pissed and talking shit? I was ready to throw in the towel, make my excuses and break the ten o'clock rule, but then it changed, as it always does, around Beer Three.

Good things really do come in threes.

Something happens on the Dad's Night around Beer Three. It is the most magnificent beer. Beer One and Two pale into comparison. They offer nothing but murmurs and silence. But Beer Three stands tall, it dives deep into the soul of a dad and looks for hope. And this night proved no different. The dads started talking, ironically, reminiscing about all the adventures they had on their previous Dad's Night. There had been others? I felt betrayed but also intrigued.

"Remember when we went to get Indian and they wouldn't serve us because we were too pissed and then John slipped them twenty quid and they let us in."

"Yeah that was mad."

"Yeah, great stuff."

"Remember when John nearly fell into that bin? Classic."

"It was close, wasn't it?"

That was a word for word account of the actual conversation, except for the use of 'John' as I have no recollection of anyone's name. While this was no 'choose your favourite kid hanging from a cliff chat' the dads were using actual words and some of them came with smiles. At this rate, I was thinking, we might become friends. And then, I undid all of Beer Three's hard work.

"I nearly fell into a bin once."

What a crime against decent conversation! Someone was telling a story about a guy who nearly fell into a bin, which is tedious enough, but desperately chiming in with 'I nearly fell into a bin' is piss-weak banter. Of all the 'I nearly's' I could've chosen. Like: 'I nearly played cricket for Australia.' Or... 'I nearly met Nelson Mandela.' Maybe... 'I nearly had an orgy with Alanis Morissette and Dido at a music festival in the 90s'. These are way better 'I nearly's' than I nearly fell into a bin. Oh God, shoot me in the face and let me survive.

The other dads nodded graciously but let me know

103

in no uncertain terms that this was John's 'nearly falling into a bin story' not mine.

"...Didn't you end up drunk in a gutter and your wife had to come and pick you up because no cab would stop?"

"Yep, I was a disgrace."

"That's what she said."

Then they all laughed and I laughed mainly because I wanted to convey the right emotion. This was Beer Three banter. Suck it, Francis, I was having fun! I think.

"Dads! Dads! Dads!" I chanted hoping to fit in. Went for nothing.

"Someone's had too many," said one of the Johns. We all laughed which was further proof we were having a good time. And that's when I figured out the rhythm of a Dad's Night.

Beer One conversation is a roll call of sorts. You drink while you wait for everyone to arrive. Beer Two conversation centres around questions about work and answers that don't take up more than a grunt or two. But Beer Three chat is where it really kicks off as the dads start talking about everything that happened on the previous Dad's Night. So where does Beer Four leave us?

Ahh, Beer Four!

Beer Four has no conversation whatsoever. I initially thought the night had gone back to the dark days of Beer One but how wrong I was. Beer Four is the set-up beer for Beers Five and Six. Beer Four is a tactical quick beer for reasons that will soon become apparent. You see Beer Three is the standout beer. The dads are desperate to lift the awkward veil of insecurity and doubt and Beer Three comes along and saves the entire night. You go into Beer Four feeling bubbly, 'We're away here, let's keep this going'. Beer Four needs to clear a path for the all-important Beer Five and Six. By the time Beer Five and Six came about we were all punching shoulders, calling each other a wanker, talking about how annoying our kids are. You'd call it fun. I smiled. At one point my knees were bopping to music in the background. Bopping! Beer Five and Six were good time brews but deep in the recesses of my mind lay a pressure.

You see during or possibly after Beer Five and Six, someone within the group must do something memorable, otherwise on the next Dad's Night, Beer Three will involve no reminiscing and the night will be over before it has even started. Clearly the moment doesn't have to be much. Nearly falling into a bin was this night's Beer Three chat. The bar wasn't high. We just needed someone to do something crazy, really break free and give the next Dad's Night some proper zing.

It had to be me.

It made perfect sense. It was my first Dad's Night which essentially made it my initiation. Maybe John was on his first night when he nearly fell into that bin? If true, he brought nothing to the table and it couldn't happen again. Being Australian didn't help my cause.

For some reason British people view Australians as rebel rousers, ready to jump into mischief and create a stir at the drop of a hat. The weight of expectation was unbearable. I had to do something stupid for my country. Had I eaten dinner before I left, I would have made better choices. I was five pints in on an empty stomach, then I was six pints in, then I was buying a round of Sambuca's... and yelling 'Our lives are more than this! Our lives are more than this!' I could've ended the night there. That would've been fine.

I don't remember saying goodbye. I know they were watching me, I could hear them laugh. Am I now mates with this mysterious group of dads called John? What did I do? Laughter is good sign surely? I'm yet to get a text message. The WhatsApp group remains silent. Have they started a new one without me? How did I get home? I'm missing a sock. I hope I didn't make too big a fool of myself. I can't move to a new town and start again, again. I need this. Lucy needs this. It's so stupid that the only way I can find out what happened is to go on the next Dad's Night and wait for the Beer Three banter where hopefully someone will be kind enough to let me know what I did.

I have to drive to Newcastle for a gig tomorrow and if my throbbing head is anything to go by, I could be in real trouble.

Hurled my guts up on the M6. No good comes from the two day hangover. Newcastle hated me, possibly more than I hated myself which says a lot given this morning I woke up punching my own face. Horrible. They booed me off the stage, then booed me back on just so they could boo me off again. The host came on after me and told the crowd that my gig was part of the Make-A-Wish Foundation and that if nothing else my actual death won't be as bad as what had just occurred. My self-esteem couldn't get much lower.

━━━━━━━━━━━━━━━━━━━━━━━

Lucy just told me none of the dads are called John.

━━━━━━━━━━━━━━━━━━━━━━━

I got home from a hard day of writing jokes about super absorbent hand towels to find Graham cleaning my windows. And that's not a euphemism, he was actually cleaning my windows. Lucy and her mum were sat in the lounge room, drinking prosecco fawning over the Welshman's hairy legs as he stood on the ladder working up his suds.

"Why is Graham cleaning our windows?" I asked in dismay.

"Isn't he brilliant?" Judy said, looking set to slide right off the sofa.

"Mum loves Graham."

"I can see. You know he's married, Judy?"

"I'm just admiring his handy work, Adam, he's very good with a sponge," she laughed.

"Graham volunteered. He was done scrubbing his and he kindly offered to scrub ours as well, ours are very dirty." Lucy and her mum looked at each other and let out a raucous laugh before returning their gaze to the window, giggling quietly into their glasses.

"I could've done the windows." That was me lying.

"Oh rubbish, you are terrified of heights. Graham on the other hand, he doesn't seem to be afraid of anything," Lucy said in her continual bid to stir me up. I refused to take the bait.

"Just don't let him bake us a pie. I've put on two kilos since he started using puff pastry."

"We'll do our best to avoid his pie. Now, don't forget we have the Lupton kid's party tomorrow afternoon."

"Isn't that a drop-off and pick up party?"

"No, it's a parents getting drunk while kids run amok party. And you're coming! You'll love it, their boy is new in Lizzie's class, they're just back from Dubai, and apparently, they're super posh."

"Don't worry, Adam, I'll be there too," Judy said raising her glass to me then turning her gaze back to Graham's crotch.

"They're making us go? On a Saturday? Well, isn't life just great!" I loped upstairs like a ten-year-old who'd just been asked to do his homework. I splayed out on the bed sulking while Graham waved at me from the other side of my freshly polished sash windows.

I've never understood the children's birthday party. We put these kids on a pedestal in front of a cake covered in flaming candles, then thirty strangers stand around and chant 'Happy Birthday' while the star of the show makes a wish by thrusting a knife into a chocolate sponge. And then we offer them up gifts! It's like an Aztec ritual except the only thing we're sacrificing is reality.

The lies we spin.

Your eighth birthday is great, you dress up as a pirate and play pass-the-parcel and somehow win the majority of the prizes. Your ninth is a repeat of your eighth only this time you're dressed as a cowboy. At your sweet sixteenth you come dressed as a Goth and the happy birthdays are now coming with a sense of concern. At your seventeenth you swap the make up for a cheap Miami Vice look, hoping your cousin will let you touch her side boob. When you turn eighteen people start calling you an adult even though you've achieved nothing. Your nineteenth is an odd fish of a birthday because you try weed for the first time and end up sitting in the corner wondering what happened to the eight-year-old you. Your twentieth has you getting dumped by Hayley Nezbit because you don't have a disposable income and hand jobs at your mum's house are starting to feel weird. Your twenty-first birthday has you surrounded by everyone who's ever known and loved you, but mainly because you promised a free bar. Your mum gets up and says some lovely words and your dad gives you one of his few public hugs before asking for you to politely fuck off and leave the family home because 'frankly it's time'. By your twenty-second birthday you're combing the classifieds for any job you can find. You have no money, no skills and crazily your 'everything has worked out thus far because people used to sing for me' personality doesn't seem to be holding much sway. Had you not smoked so much weed on your nineteenth birthday maybe you would have stayed at university. Now you're celebrating your twenty second birthday by taking any job you can find. Unluckily for you the only job you can find is that of a children's party entertainer. Ain't that a kick in the teeth? Having to go back to the very parties that boosted your hopes in the first place only this time you're dressed as Wilky The Wizard. Who is Wilky The Wizard? Exactly! No one knows. Why? Because rather than paying for the licence fee to use the superheroes that kids actually wanted to see, your new employers decided to circumvent these payments by inventing a low rent dipshit of a wizard.

Now, it's the eve of your twenty third birthday and you've spent nearly a year arriving at strange houses dressed up as an unknown wizard, a wizard with no backstory, a wizard with a barn storming hangover, a wonky wizard, a wizard who had he applied himself would have been an engineer by now, a regretful wizard, a wizard that once forgot his spare set of clothes and had to catch the train dressed as a wizard, wizard, a wizard who wanted to be a comedian but didn't know how wizard, a wizard who could barely pay rent entertaining five year olds all of whom were off their chops on sherbet and Fruit Tingles. That kind of wizard. Twelve months of hell! Every other out of work wannabe comic and actor was dressing up as Superman or The Hulk or Thor. It was high fives all round for those well-known pricks. Yet here you are in the pre-Harry Potter post Merlin driest ever patch for wizards year of 1996, having to make other people's children happy by dressing up as a wand carrying purple smock wearing pointy hatted newbie fuckhead. Carnage! Kicked in the balls, spat on, scratched, locked in laundry rooms, humped by schnauzers and pass-the-parcelled to within in an inch of your sad diabolical existence. So yeah, fuck birthdays!

My children don't get a party. I refuse. They can choose two mates and we head to Pizza Express for three slices of whatever you fancy and a muffin. Everyone walks away happy. And I always follow the universal rule that is, the parents of the kid invited must buy your kid twenty pounds worth of useless junk and in return you look after their child for no more or no less than two hours. Standard! And you never invite the parents. Ever! In a perfect world you ask if their siblings would like to tag along so the parents of the invitees can go home and enjoy a daytime shag. The nerve of the Luptons asking us over for a 'get together' so we can celebrate the anniversary of another human being falling out of a vagina. I despair.

I let out a giant whistle, the kind that only arrives when you've seen or heard something suitably shocking. You see the Grand Canyon, you whistle, your mate loses his shirt at the track, you whistle, you walk into The Luptons' joint, you whistle.

"This is how you do it," said Judy, looking at me with her usual 'lift your game face'. She knew this world better than most. Judy was born with a silver spoon in her horse's mouth. Life may have left her poor but this was her turf.

"These Luptons are posh. I should've clocked it when we were asked to use the side entrance. Isn't that the first rule of being rich, Judy? Don't risk the parquetry on the plebs. Hopefully by the end of the day we'll have earnt front door privileges," I said with a wry smile.

"I doubt you'll see their boot room, Adam," another snide pop from Judy, completely forgetting she lived under my roof.

"Kids, don't break anything..." Albie and Lizzie were off before Lucy finished the sentence... "Don't you break anything either," she said elbowing me in the ribs before taking her mum's hand and walking proudly into the swank.

Their garden must have been three hundred feet long and a hundred wide. It was covered in lush green grass, the kind you see at Lords on the first day of an Ashes Test. It was beautiful. A paved patio three times the size of our house held a jacuzzi, a foosball table, a table tennis table and a table with a two-man catering team who were dishing out Indian food to whoever wanted it. Wowsers! You know that game where you ask 'what you'd do if you won a million dollars?', well this backyard was what you would do if you won ten times that. Waiters carried around trays of Champagne that you could just take and if you preferred beer, they had a fully stocked bar set to one side. In the middle of that sumptuous soft lawn stood the posh man's beacon, the white marquee. Another whistle. All the older folk who couldn't handle the heat from what was an unusually warm summers day were perched underneath chomping into their strawberries and cream. A banner reading Happy Birthday Thomas stretched across its entrance with large bunches of weighted helium balloons either side. Little Tommy was well heeled. To your left you had a vegetable patch sprouting rhubarb and corn and beans and tomatoes. Lush. They clearly have a green thumb, probably from paying their gardener in cash. This was a professionally manicured patch. On the right side of their 'too good to be true ' garden stood a life-sized statue of a mother holding a boy who pissed water into a tranquil pond, edged with geraniums. At the back of the garden was a chicken coup. These people were living on a country estate in the middle of Bedford. Their 'piece de resistance' was a giant eighteen-foot-high bronzed statue of a giraffe that stood behind the pond. No wonder the kid was pissing.

Children frolicked up and down the garden playing tag, skipping in and around the adults but never enough to annoy. I saw babies but heard no crying, mums but no gossip, dads were using more than two syllables. There was laughter yet no one person was holding court, conversations were flowing naturally, everyone seemingly interested in what the other had to say, it was all so amiable. The Luptons really had brought a touch of class to the Reception year party set. And I had them down as selfish boring arseholes when maybe, just maybe, they were rich, warm and generous. Maybe? I stood to the side and took it all in, giddy with delight knowing that I had an afternoon of free food, plenty of booze and an opportunity to really examine this all too pleasant narrative. It wasn't just the garden that made me smell horse shit. I'd been to enough birthday parties to know that no normal parents put on a soiree with full catering and a marquee for a five-year-old. Maybe in the Hamptons but not in Bum-fuck-Bedford. Somewhere behind this happy family stood some proper deep-seated pain, a mistress being shagged here, a gardener being seduced there, maybe they had a demented child living in the attic, or a dead body under the vegetable patch? The rhubarb was unusually bright. Who knew? I knocked back a passing flute of bubbly and strolled into the fray like Johnny Good times determined to find out.

I was on fire.

The Hinkletons loved my impersonation of a Judge ordering hors d'oeuvres.

"Hors d'oeuvres! Hors d'oeuvres in the court! Hors d'oeuvres in the garden!"

I did a two-step with one of the nans. I'm pretty sure I saw all the mums looking at me thinking, "That guy is a bit of all right."

I met a bloke called, Craig. He and I were instant besties.

"Tell me, Craig, we both have kids here and we love them dearly but would you ever put on a spread of this magnitude?"

"Not a chance in hell!"

"Exactly! Thank you, mate, it's too much. Don't get me wrong, I'll drink their Champagne and these salmon croutons are exquisite but where does poor Thomas go from here?"

"How's the giraffe?"

"Oh mate, I've made some drunk eBay purchases

in my time but that is next level. How many of your life goals have you achieved before a bronze statue of a giraffe feels like a necessary purchase? What's on the list? House, car, new kitchen, holiday… life sized bronzed statue of a giraffe? Where does that fit on your hierarchy of needs?"

"Third."

"Ha yes, I had mine at fourth but only because we're still due a kitchen. We have to ride it, mate, you can't put an eighteen-foot giraffe in your backyard, hand out free booze and not expect people to jump on."

"Their kids are off to private school next year so you may as well, they won't look at us twice after today."

"Private school? Well, la-di-da."

"La! Di! Da!" Craig belted, turning the odd head.

"Craig, you are my spirit animal!"

Craig beat his chest like a gorilla which nearly made me cry because finally someone got me. I'd had eight years of stifled dad chats, small talk with shop keepers, run-ins with the neighbours but I'd never made an instant connection. Was today the day that me and this town finally turned a corner? It would have been, had the Champagne not played havoc with my bladder.

"Hold that thought, Craig, I have to hang a slash but more good times are heading your way."

And with that, I was off. The party was so big I was consumed by it. I nodded and helloed my way to the back door, looking for the toilet. Lucy and Judy stopped me on the way through.

"All OK, honey?" asked Lucy, probably with a concerned frown, hard to tell as I was half-cut at the time.

"I'm brilliant, I've met someone, Craig is his name. I'm looking for a toilet. How's the giraffe?"

"I like it. Simone told me Jeremy got it for her birthday."

"Jeremy is a stock broker, Adam... maybe you should ask him for some tips."

"Good idea, Judy. I tell you what, why don't you..."

"Toilets are through the kitchen and on the left," Lucy said, averting what could have been a rather lippy tete-a-tete.

"Thanks, honey. You happy?"

"I'm nervous, I know that look in your eye."

"I'm on my best behaviour, but right now Niagara Falls wants to burst through my strides."

And with that I walked into the kitchen and followed a sign that said 'Toilet This Way' with an arrow that lead me to a closed door.

"Busy," was the response.

"Righto." I waited but the pressure was mounting. I peered through the adjacent door. It was the bathroom. Of course, rich people don't shit in the same room as their toothbrush. It's uncouth. I knocked on the toilet door to move things along but was met with a much sterner "Busy!" so really I had no choice.

I locked the bathroom door behind me, undid my belt, tried not to catch my face in the cabinet mirror and unleashed a torrent of highly filtered Champagne into the hand basin. I aimed for the drain to avoid splash back and also soften the sound of my piss bouncing off the porcelain. Is there anything better than a good wee? I stood there pissing for what felt like minutes before hearing the flush of a toilet and then I got my own knock on the door. "Busy," I said desperately trying to hurry things along. A woman's voice shot through the door, "I need to wash my hands." Still pissing I began sucking in the wee fumes hoping to rid the room of my stench but the asparagus dip I'd eaten twenty minutes earlier was taking no prisoners. With one hand on my Boris Johnson, I used the other to open the cabinet in the hope of finding some kind of perfume to hide my scent. Vera Wang! These people spare no expense. Very posh and oddly pertinent. Three squirts of old Vera did the trick but not before I spotted two boxes of Viagra. Bingo! That explained the giraffe. Compensation for the dong pills. Another knock.

"Coming!"

I tapped out, zipped up and opened the door only to see a lady with a cranky face in a canary yellow shirt staring me down. I had no desire to go toe to toe with Big Bird.

"Sorry, I had trouble putting in my contacts." And with that I ducked under her wing, rushed back through the kitchen and into the safety of the garden where I was pounced on by Albie.

"Dad! Can Paulie and I have a play date?"

"Sure, quick let's move away from the house." I hurried through the crowd keen to put distance between me and the bathroom.

"Yes!" Albie and his little mate did a shimmy, so I wasn't really sure what I had just agreed to. I was more focussed on blending in which became a lot easier when the parents of Albie's little mate arrived on the scene. Both older with beetroot red faces, they were quite rotund and thus very easy to hide behind.

"Hello, you must be Albie's father?"

"What's he done now?" I exaggerated for comical effect. Got fuck all.

"Oh, nothing. Paulie is forever mentioning your boy Albie, so it's good to finally meet his dad? This is my wife Jan."

"Paulie and Albie, isn't it cute? Do you mind if I give Albie a bag of sweets?" asked Jan with a directness that suggested she suffered from a heavy dose of Asperger's.

Albie and this Paulie kid, who was also a tad on the chunky side, yelled out, "Sweets!" and did another shimmy. In a half-pickled state I had to make a parenting decision. I hate it when other grownups do this. You never ask for a parent's permission in front of the child. Massive faux pas! If I say 'no' they've now made me the arsehole. It's basic manners.

"It's just a bag of party sweets," sighed Jan's

husband who was clearly some kind of county lines sugar dealer.

"Please, Dad, can I?" Albie really worked on his ski jump eye brows when asking. Manipulative skills he got from his mother.

"Sure, go for it, have a bag of sugar. Hey Jan, tell me… if your boy comes over for a play date is it OK if I put him on a treadmill? He looks a bit chubby and unruly for my liking, maybe he could jog it off?"

"Excuse me?"

"I said isn't this a great kid's party." And with that I shot off not wanting to witness Albie's imminent sugar high.

I spent the next hour looking for my new mate Craig but he was nowhere to be seen, so I hit the free bar, flirted with the grandmas and made inappropriate jokes with the grandpas. There were no awkward moments. Judy was also in fine form hobnobbing with the well-to-dos. Lucy was in deep talks with Canary Yellow (yikes), while Lizzie was teaching the other kids how to do cartwheels. Albie had hooked up with his new best friend, the sugar rush. They laughed and danced and cheered and sang songs that made no sense. I imagine it was one of the greatest afternoons of his life. Forget the whining, the not wanting to eat dinner and the bedtime hysterics, other than these trivial events my boy had a great party. I have to take credit for most of the fun though because the day really took off once I got to play DJ.

Sometimes you can just tell when a group of people are ready to up the good time vibe and jump on the happy train. Most of the folks were chirpy and a buzz was definitely about, but I could feel the collective subconscious of this mob wanting more. I don't know if it was the positioning of the sun, or the slight breeze in the unusually warm air, or if it was the abundance of free booze, but in that garden, on that day, at that time, this otherwise ordinary bunch of Bedfordians were ready to turn one on. We were gagging for it. Our only barrier to spontaneous joy was Billie Eilish. Whoever put her on the play list should have been sent to the Hague for crimes against fun. This party needed a tune. If not me, who? If not now, when?

I found a speaker and followed the lead which ran across the front of the patio. I must have been a sight, the tipsy drunken dad bent over like an emu searching amongst the hibiscus for the end of his musical tether. My scrounging wasn't in vain however, as the wire led to yet another table and behind that table stood two angsty young girls hunched over an iPhone.

"I was wondering if I could play a couple of songs, I'm a friend of Mr Lupton and he's requested I put on a few of our old favourites."

"You mean, Dad? His music? No way," said the girl, who despite being half my size still managed to look down on me.

"He also told me that Thomas is in your bedroom with his mates, so if you had anything to hide, best get him out."

"In my bedroom? That little weasel!" And with that, the two girls were off. I plugged in my phone ready to light up the afternoon.

I started with The Beach Boys' Good Vibrations, because it does what it says on the tin. It only took a few verses and the good vibrations started flowing. With everyone's shoulders now relaxed I went rogue and popped on Manfred Mann's Do Wah Diddy Diddy... A bold choice, a brave choice, but sometimes in life you have to put your balls on the line.

"There she was just a walking down the street singing..." I walked out into the middle of the garden and belted out. "...Do wah diddy diddy dum diddy do" with complete abandon but not much uptake. Lizzie ran past, so I grabbed her and we started dancing.

"Snappin' her fingers and..."

"... shuffling her feet!" My spirit animal, Craig, came in with the save. Now we were two pissed dads. Two more, and we were halfway to a choir.

'Singing Do wah diddy diddy dum diddy do!' Thankfully more merriment came to the rescue... by the third verse there must have been twenty of us just going for it. Nannas were up shaking their good hips, some of the dads went arm in arm, the mums stood by for a while but once a few joined in, they all did. Then the entire garden found its flow. The kids went absolutely troppo, they didn't even know the words but their little limbs were flying everywhere. Heads were shaking, feet were tapping, the congregation was spellbound. I've never heard 'Do wah diddy diddy dum diddy do!' sung with such gusto. People were dancing and kissing, it was uninhibited visceral joy, it was magic! Like we'd just won the war. A loud 'fuck you' to all the cool kids of London, to the daily commute, to the humdrum, to the grey drizzle, to the worry, to the monotony of our sluggish suburban lives. We were in it! I sang my way back to the table ready to bring us home. And when Oasis' Don't Look Back In Anger came on you would've been able to hear us from Luton. There must have been fifty of us, each a stranger to the other, all swinging arm in arm howling away at the daytime moon. It was the best half an hour of Bedford's existence. Then Craig, climbed the giraffe.

As a rule, you should never climb a bronzed giraffe. By all means look at it, pat it if you must, but avoid mounting it, especially at birthdays. Craig was on the back of the giraffe singing away, arms in the air, like he was front and centre at the main stage at Glastonbury. We locked eyes and even though we'd only just met, I gave him the two-armed salute, that one gives to a mate they haven't seen in ages. My new friend and I had connected. Now, I don't know if the moment had taken him or if he was trying to impress me, but as I raised my arms up in triumph Craig started scooching further up the bronzed animal's neck and the higher he climbed the more precarious it looked. Then, the giraffe started moving.

"Craig! Craig!" My cries were of no use, everyone was singing at the top of their lungs. Poor Craig was teetering on disaster about to land giraffe-head-first into two mums, one nana and a baby.

"Everyone out of the way!" I yelled and shooed with my arms wide as if to scare off a bear. People scurried away desperate to avoid disaster while the bronze beast lost its moorings and sank headfirst into the marquee. I dived onto Craig to try and break his fall only to be swamped by canvas. The marque was all around us. The joyous singing was replaced with screaming and tears.

"I'm pinned! I'm pinned!" Craig's right leg was firmly under the giraffe. A few of the other dads and I helped set him free.

"It's all right, foot's not broken," Craig announced happily, not appreciating the gravity of the situation.

"Not broken? Not Broken? You broke the whole bloody day." Canary Yellow stood at the edge of the now very much collapsed marquee, as the party formed a circle around a fumbling Craig. I tried to extract myself from their wrath by slowly army rolling off to one side. Lucy and her mum were not impressed when I ended up at their feet. I copped a swift foot to the ribs from Lucy.

"Get up," she said under her breath.

"Daddy!" At least Elizabeth was happy to see me. Albie did his best to divert attention by beating the giraffe's head with his shoe, like it was a fallen Saddam

Hussein statue.

"Is everyone OK?" I said out loud, like I hadn't been a big part of the problem.

One can only assume it was Mr Lupton who told Craig he had to leave.

"Yep, that seems fair… sorry." And with that the poor man uprighted one of the many fallen chairs, and hobbled off down the side of the house. The mob's eyes followed him out, the social pariah, the limpy leper who would never again be welcome into the upper echelons of Bedford's Reception year party scene. There was tutting, eye rolling and a lot of men with their shoulders arched back ready for biff should they be called upon. Canary Yellow, still seething behind a forced smile, tried to save what was left of the party, "Okay, people, shall we do the birthday cake? Cake sounds good, doesn't it? Cake!"

Say what you want about the Brits, but a soft moist slice of Victoria sponge really lifts their spirits. Had the French been so easy to please, Mary Antoinette might have kept her noggin. The marquee was quickly folded up and packed away, while a few of the dads hoisted the giraffe back into its original position. The tables and chairs were put back in place. All memory of Craig's downfall had been quickly erased and forgotten. Nearly.

Lucy firmly whispered, "We're leaving!"

"What about the cake?" My question fell on deaf ears. Judy was rounding up the kids and making her way out. Albie looked confused. "But we haven't done the cake." In his defence, a squashed clump of cake in a bag with a shitty 'thank you' toy is the universal signal that a kid's party has officially come to an end. Leaving without singing Happy Birthday is sacrilegious. But so is being slung over your grandma's shoulder and trotted out to the car.

"What's the rush?" I said to Lucy, a bit flummoxed.

"You're pissed."

"I'm toasty. I'm also the reason this place was jumping."

"Yes, you got it so riled up even the giant giraffe got involved. Someone could've been killed."

"I didn't put the giraffe there. You know that Lupton fella is on Viagra."

"What?" Lucy was now the flummoxed one.

His ears must have been burning because Mr Lupton tapped me on the shoulder, "Excuse me, I think you forgot your phone. My daughter tells me that you and I are old friends."

Bugger, he had me, and he knew it.

"Yes, I may have stretched the friendship on that one but Billie Eilish songs do bring out the worst in me, *When the Party's Over* is a bad omen for a sunny day in Bedford." The blank look on Mr Lupton's face told me he wasn't familiar with Billie's work. Half his luck.

"Have we met?"

"No, I don't think I've had the pleasure, although I will say you really put on a rock solid party, you were a bit stiff with the marquee falling down, but we've all

126

had a few beers and suffered from a droopy marquee, haven't we?"

"That's right, you're the Australian chap from the Dad's Night. Adam, isn't it?" Oh shit, the Dad's Night. I thought this was a different group of kids with a different group of parents.

"Yes… Hi John…?" Lucy elbowed me in the guts.

"Jeremy," said the man who was not called John.

"Right, of course, Jeremy… how could I forget? Tell me… Jeremy… what happened at the end of that Dad's Night? I woke up wearing one sock… I can't remember a damn thing!"

"Oh, I wasn't there, I've just heard that it was a very interesting night. Lucy, it was lovely to meet you," said the smug prick as he placed his hand on her shoulder. Power move.

"Yes, sorry about the… everything," Lucy said, blushing.

"Before I go, Jeremy, how do you get the grass so perfectly green?" I asked.

"Trade secret," he said, with a fuck you smile.

And with that Lucy grabbed my hand and dragged me out to the street. We had officially departed the great House of Lupton. We walked silently towards the car and as soon as we were away from earshot, my lovely wife unloaded.

"What is wrong with you?"

"Nothing!"

"You've humiliated me, Mum, yourself! The kids

127

will never get invited to a party again. I can't do this, Adam, I can't."

"I'm fine. You're blowing it way out of proportion."

"What happened between you and Simone?"

"Who?"

"Jeremy's other half!"

"Oh, Canary Yellow, nothing happened. Why?"

"She tells me there was an incident in the bathroom."

Vera Wang was useless! Five minutes earlier I had instigated one of the greatest garden party sing-a-longs Bedford had ever seen. Now my wife was looking at me wondering why a woman would complain about me in the bathroom. I'd gone from a brilliant DJ to a sex pest, which unfortunately isn't an unheard of transition in this country. Still, it's one I'd rather avoid.

"I may have pissed in their sink…"

Lucy gasped. "Get in the car!"

"Don't speak to me like I'm five." I got in the car.

"What's he done now?" Judy said with an already disgusted tone.

"I haven't done anything, Judy, actually, so maybe you could… relax."

"He pissed in their sink."

"Jesus, Adam!" Judy's 'Jesus' came from deep down, the world hadn't heard a 'Jesus' like that since the fifties.

"Don't sound so shocked, Judy, there must have

been a hundred people there with only one toilet. It's basic biology and maths, that's all."

"It's disgusting, that's what it is!" Lucy was livid.

"Were there other dads there from the Dad's Night?"

"There may have been one or two, I don't know, I'm not the keeper of the dads. But for the last time, none of them were called John!"

Lucy started the car and sped us off home. We drove in silence past a still limping Craig. I tried to meet his gaze but his eyes were cast firmly on the pavement. His wife and kids walked ten yards ahead but he was very much alone. The poor bastard. Just more proof that life could always get worse.

Later that night, after finally getting Albie to bed, I lay uncomfortably on the couch staring at the ceiling waiting for my three *a.m.* piss, humming away to Bedford's favourite tune, 'Do wah diddy diddy dum diddy do'. You couldn't wipe the smile from my face.

Lucy is still annoyed that I pissed in the Luptons' hand basin. It's hard to know if she's annoyed or jealous? Not everyone can do it.

I fell asleep in front of the TV last night. I woke up at 1 in the morning with Glen's face on the screen staring right at me. He was selling robot vacuum cleaners. I only wrote that one last week.

"Open the box, turn it on and your carpets will be cleaned twenty-four-seven. It uses an algorithm designed specifically to clean your entire house. I don't know what that means. I'm bad at maths and the wife did say I had no rhythm. Algo-Rhythm, get it? (Glen puts a rose between his teeth and dances with the robotic vacuum cleaner under a spotlight. He continues to camera). This device could save your marriage, had I bought my wife one of these... she wouldn't have run off with the cleaner. Honey, if you're watching, I hope Michelle was worth it. So, get a vacuum cleaner that only has eyes for the job. And all for the low, low price of three hundred pounds. And the best bit is, when you're *out* your new cleaner will be *in*, working tirelessly on *your* carpet. Again, big shout out to Michelle."

It was completely stupid and hackie but somehow, Glen made it work.

━━━━━━━━━━━━━━━━━━

We're getting ready for the build.

The fact that Lucy has so easily managed to turn my sitting-room-office into a makeshift kitchen makes me wonder why we're spending so much money putting in a new one. I'm surrounded by butter, long-life milk, biscuits, spiral-pasta, half a carton of eggs and four tins of chopped tomatoes. And the Vera Wang incident still has me lying on the outer rim of the mattress. Nothing about my life is comfortable.

Judy moving into the loft has taken out the last viable room, the kids have been granted squatters rights in the lounge, even the shoes and coats get under the stairs privileges. Injustice makes me hungry and here I am surrounded by snacks. If the cost of this new kitchen doesn't kill me type two diabetes might.

Got a voice message from Glen.

"Mate, these TV cunts are getting killed by the fuck'n internet. That's why they come to us because we fuck'n make this shit exciting. So, I need eight rip roaring gags about fuck'n worm farms. Briefs in your inbox, send 'em when you got 'em. See ya, cunt!"

Translation.

Hello Adam, TV is a dying medium so don't expect this job to be around too much longer. I've had to resort to selling worm farms late at night. Can you create some humorous situation to help me look like less of a prick? I've emailed you through an offer on the money, please accept or we'll both be out of a job. All the best. Glen.

Big morning for the street, three doors up got robbed while they slept. It caused quite the stir at Kevin and Sylvia's house. They're a strange couple. Kevin hides behind financial magazines and Apple products hoping the world doesn't recognise he married Sylvia for her cash. Kevin's not a bad bloke, good for a nod when you stroll past his window, but he does nothing during the day which can't be great for his self-esteem, as he's still in his thirties plus Sylvia is at least fifteen years his senior. Gross. The chuckle I get from knowing he married old Sylvia for her old Sylvia can get me through the rough days. She drives him around town in her Audi waving to whoever will notice. I sometimes think Kevin believes he's in love, but then I'll see him through their front window and he looks as if he's trapped in a double glazed coffin, like a nineteen fifties housewife. He'll read the Financial Times thinking he's some kind of high-rolling stockbroker, even wearing ridiculous looking braces as if he's on Wall Street. I like to yell 'Sell, mate, sell!' as I walk past his house, but if last night's robbery is anything to go by Kevin never hears me.

We were all woken up at the crack of dot to Sylvia's screaming. Being good neighbours, we ran out to see what the fuss was about. Six of us there in our pyjamas ready to get involved with Warwick Avenue's latest commotion. Kevin and Sylvia met us on their front doorstep shaking, waiting for the police to arrive. All they wanted from us was a chance to run through all of their high-end goods that had been flogged.

Sylvia really turned on the tears, "They took my diamonds! My De Beers!"

Kevin wasn't to be outdone, "My MacBook Pro is missing. It was top of the range."

Sylvia went up an octave, "All of my mother's silverware."

Kevin didn't back down, "My iPad's gone, only got it last month. They won't be able to use it, facial recognition."

Sylvia again, "They took a crystal vase." Side note, some of the other gear got a few ooh's and ah's but no one gave two shits about her crystal.

Kevin held up his empty wrist, "Where's my Apple Watch? The one night I leave it downstairs. The last three months of my sleeping patterns… lost."

"At least they're backed up in the cloud, not like my Gucci handbag," said a crying Sylvia with one eye on our reaction.

The despair on Sylvia's face wasn't enough to disguise the obvious glee she got from reeling off her favourite stolen goods. All the while being held by her most prized possession, Kevin.

"The good news is you weren't hurt," said a familiar thick Welsh accent. Bloody Graham. Unbelievable! A gaudy woman in her mid-fifties entraps a weasel of a man in his mid-thirties, screams to get the attention of the street at six a.m., gloats about her stolen jewels and still Graham manages to find the positives. He was wrong, these people were not only hurting, they were broken. Poor Kevin was totally dead behind the eyes, which is what happens when you marry the wrong woman.

I was all set to head back to the comfort of my couch for another hour of shut-eye when from the back of our neighbourly pack came…

"Bob down the road got done." It came from Sally!

Sally wasn't new to announcements. Word has it that she spent her twenties calling the weather for BBC Local News and another five doing traffic reports on Three Counties Radio. For over two decades old Sal flew above the people of Bedfordshire letting them know why they weren't getting anywhere. A short woman with a thinning bouffant of bright pink helicopter hair, her smile looked more like a 'Go Fuck Yourself'. What's more impressive is she hadn't uttered a word in ten years, so the announcement of Bob getting done came with some real gravitas. All of us were wondering the same thing, but were too afraid to ask, then Judy arrived having just got back from her morning walk, "Who's Bob? And what do you mean he got done?"

"Bob has lived down the road for thirty-five years and they got him last week. He's a mess. Robbed him blind. We've seen a spate of burglaries in the area. If any of you bothered to read the Bedford Clanger you'd know." And with that Sally turned her slippers back into the direction of her house and strolled on home, smiling the whole way no doubt.

Everyone started muttering, "Bob down the road got done," in bewildered tones before turning around and doing the same.

Sylvia tried to reel us back in, "I think they stole a case of wine." But it was over. The avenue suddenly felt vulnerable.

I took Sally's advice and bought the latest copy of The Clanger. The classifieds are good for a chuckle.

'For Sale: One vintage iron decorative milking bucket, good condition yet to be kicked, thirty pounds.'

Another.

'Used chicken coup doesn't come with chickens – they crossed the road, yet to find out why.'

Little ticklers that get you through the day.

In other news, the family car is now my new office. Too much noise from the builders and they were rubbish at generating ideas. "Got any jokes on worm farms lads?" They couldn't even offer up a half-baked premise. All they had were doubts that my job existed and a sudden desire to get paid upfront.

Last night I did a gig in Colchester and really had fun. Thank God they enjoyed my story about the Luptons. I needed a good one. My last three gigs have been absolute dogs but this made me feel funny again. I got home at one *a.m.* and snuck into bed which was no mean feat given my aching back. It's my ego versus my body and both are losing to my bills. I hobbled down for breakfast around eight only to discover four blokes with hard hats preparing to knock out my kitchen wall.

Workmen! My nemesis! Noise dust and testosterone.

I love nothing more than watching strong able-bodied men with calloused hands walking around with heavy hammers, drilling holes into my wife's old kitchen while asking her if she's happy with how things are going. It fills me with joy! They never ask me if I'm happy. 'Forget about that useless excuse for a man he's just the one paying for it.' I can feel their judgement. They think I'm a slacker. I work just as hard as they do. Sitting in the front seat of my Hyundai because it's the only free space I can find, writing jokes about worm farms isn't easy, but I do it. Why? Because late night TV demands it! That's why! I may not knock down adjoining walls for a living but not many people can break down the intricacies of a five stacker compost system and then turn that information into entertainment. That takes years of practice. It's just as rewarding as installing a twenty-six-cupboard kitchen with a worktop and five ring range cooker. If you put garden waste in the ground it turns into methane which kills the ozone layer, but if you let compost worms break that waste down, it turns into soil. So, if I do my job right, people buy more worm farms, which rids the world of more methane, which saves the planet. We've all done our bit. These workmen aren't the only ones who get to stand back and go 'wow'.

Plus, last night I did a gig in Colchester and made one hundred and eight pounds. Given these builders are going to see a hundred and eight of those pounds they should show me some goddamn respect.

One of the builders gave me dirty looks as he carried my old sink to the skip out front. I showed my disdain by turning my windscreen wipers on.

Lucy pointed out I'm speaking half an octave lower than usual. She thinks I act manlier when surrounded by other men. I asked her what time dinner would be ready. We laughed. This new kitchen may be putting me back in the good books.

First thing this morning I walked down the stairs to find Judy in her familiar position, standing in the bay of the lounge room eating a bowl of porridge, staring out the window. The semi rhythmic clang of spoon hitting plate combined with her chewing as the morning light seeped into the room was somehow comforting. What a life she must have lived. Born rich, married richer, then lost the lot trying to save her husband's property portfolio. Now she's practically penniless yet she still gets up every morning to see what's what. You had to admire her spirit.

"This town has gone to the dogs," she said still starring out the window and also scratching a big black line across the nice picture I had painted.

"Jesus, Judy…" I said startled. "…You've only been here two months, it can't have changed that much."

"Have you read the Clanger?"

Judy pointed to a copy of the local paper that was on the couch. There, on the front cover in big bold writing, *Will They Catch the Bedroom Burglar?*

"It's just the local rag trying to sell advertising, ignore it, although I do think we should look at getting chickens."

"Chickens? We need to get toothbrushes."

"What? Why toothbrushes?"

"They shove them up their bums, Adam."

OK, so, for real, my dear mother-in-law has got it into her head that Bedford's criminal mastermind is shoving peoples' toothbrushes up his or her dot and then putting them back on the bathroom shelf while his or her victims will remain none the wiser. You know, for kicks.

"You can't be too careful, Adam. These people are perverted. Toothbrushes, cutlery, if it fits, they'll stick it up there. Then six weeks later you develop your photos and there they are, right up a stranger's wazoo. First, they steal from you then they put their butt in your mouth."

"Jesus, Judy, no one is shoving cutlery up their ass. OK? No one is doing that. It's an urban myth. Plus, people haven't been developing photos for about twenty years."

"Maybe he's taking bum photos with a plan to pop them on Insta-face. You don't know how these people work. You keep the old brush only to discover three months later you've gone viral."

"Insta-face? Bum photos? Judy, no one is throwing silverware up their jacksy mid heist. OK? It's not a thing."

"That's easy for you to say, you don't have any silverware."

It always amazes me how Judy never runs out of ways to point out that I'm not good enough for her daughter. In her deranged mind, me not earning enough money to pay for shelve-able teaspoons is even more evidence that Lucy has married a loser. I can't compete with that.

"Did you see that a mob of Gypsies have moved in next door?" Judy asked, clearly hearing the bell for round two.

"Yes, I noticed we had new neighbours but Gina tells me they're from Syria, Judy, and we call 'Gypsies' Roma now. The term 'Gypsies' is frowned upon."

"Well, if the Bedford Burglar won't steal from you the bloody Roma will. And how much do you trust Gina? She's very Asian."

If nothing else Judy was proof that words aren't nearly as racist as tone.

"Gina is from India, Judy, so yes Asian, and as far as I can tell a good landlord but feel free to get all your racism out before the kids wake up. I don't want them catching it."

"We'll see… Right… I'm off, it's abs day. Let me know if you want any lessons." And with that Judy left the room patting me on the stomach, cackling her way up the stairs. She knows I don't really care what a sixty-eight-year-old lady thinks and I know that taking pot shots at me keeps her alive. I should probably ask her to stop. Judy was right about us having new neighbours though. I saw them arrive yesterday as I peered through the rear vision mirror of my new office. The poor people looked shell-shocked. Mum and Dad had that thousand-yard stare you see in the movies, the kids were all smiles but no shoes. They huddled in the courtyard next to our house scared to venture onto the footpath. Gina, the quiet Indian landlord, lives in one of the flats and rents the other two out as multi occupancy homes. Every few months a new family blows in. We've been neighbours to Poles, Russians then Ukrainians (awkward change over), there was a family from Iraq, one family was from Lebanon. It's very confronting seeing how some people live, how poor they are, yet how grateful they are to be in a country that is relatively safe and prosperous. It's even more confronting watching them do their level best to move away, because despite their horrible history, they think our street is a bit shit.

Had to do the tennis-run tonight. I got there early to check in on Albie's progress. We've spent a few hundred on it now, so I expected to see a great deal of improvement. Still hits it out. Struggles to serve. I don't know how Garry Foxe lives with himself. Where is the value for money?

There was a new dad there with his kid, getting sold down the river just like we had been two months prior. Up against some easily beatable nuff making the dad think his child has skills. These commuter belt coaches have access to a long line of gullible loser parents who are bored senseless in the burbs and are willing to throw money at the mere whiff of a chance to escape. They think if they throw some coin at their child's forehand, they'll be spending next summer in California eating strawberries with Serena Williams. And Garry plays all the old favourites. He raises his eyebrows whenever the kid hits it in, when a serve lands he gives the dad a thumbs up, and boy does he love a big exhale when the little fella hits a winner. The kid up the other end looks like he just got out of callipers but the dad doesn't care because in his mind, he's one win away from upping sticks to Malibu.

The workmen dump loads of rubble into a skip parked in front of my office. I can feel their judgement. They have no appreciation for what I do. How would I tell them?

"Hey guys, it may look like I'm a lazy douche who sits in his car hiding from life, but your wages are very much dependant on my ability to make worm farms interesting."

It didn't help today when Graham knocked on the passenger window holding a thermos wanting to chat.

I had to go through the rigmarole of turning the car on so I could lower the window.

"You OK, Graham?"

"I saw you from the window eating a sandwich and I thought, 'there's a man who needs a hot cup of cocoa'." Graham stood there holding his two cups and thermos as another bucket load of dust floated across the car and into the now open window.

"Get in," I said, mainly to prevent more dirt flying into my office but also because I didn't want to waste petrol. Graham clambered in, unscrewed his thermos and started pouring.

"Ahh so this is where the magic happens? Show biz."

"Are you takin' the piss?"

"No I mean it, I know the car isn't where you want your office to be but for me, the chance to be around the creative mind is very exciting."

"You are taking the piss."

"Not at all..." He was, his smile was a dead giveaway. "... It's not often I get the day off and what better way to spend it than hanging out with a new friend."

"I've known you for eight years, Graham, and not once have we ever so much as gone out for a beer, now you want to be Thelma to my Louise."

"I meant my thermos, Adam..." His grin was now a proper smirk. "... A pound on eBay."

"You bought a second hand thermos?"

"Times are tough, I'm down to a four day week, Judy tells me you're writing jokes about worm farms, your office is your car for Pete's sake, we all know you can't afford this new kitchen, Adam, there's a WhatsApp group specifically set up to discuss when we think you'll be selling. I've put a fiver you'll be out in six months. Don't get me wrong. I applaud the attempt. It's very courageous. All I'm saying is maybe drinking cheap cocoa from a second-hand thermos is where you, and I, are at?"

Graham took a sip of his hot cocoa and I did the same. Then he burst into laughter.

"Of course, I'm taking the piss! What has become of us? You've turned your car into your office? What a state! But I can't talk, I wash your windows because I go crazy not working. My daughter hates me, she calls me Graham which really gets my goat, plus Jess, her mother, my wife, is angry because I never started my own business and now, we can't afford holidays."

"You can't afford holidays? I thought you were Bedford's favourite plumber?"

"Well, if I was, your builder would be hiring me to work on your kitchen."

"Good point, but you're Mr Perfect, everyone loves you."

"Did you not hear me say that my daughter hates me?"

"Lucy has barley spoken to me all week."

"What for?"

"Pissed in Mrs Lupton's hand basin."

"Haha, brilliant! I see your silent treatment and raise you three sexless months."

"Ouch."

"I have my eyes on your mother-in-law."

"Judy? You're joking?"

"Of course, I'm joking!"

"Good, because she would break you in half."

"And I would let her. Is it weird, I'm attracted to a woman in her late sixties?"

"Maybe you should ask Kevin?"

"What is going on with that boy? She must be nearly sixty."

It only took eight years but we were away. Graham and I parked in my office and nattered for hours. We covered everything: work, life, death, potholes, our mutual admiration for Bred and Tender, I genuinely feel as though we are now friends. God, we had a laugh. I'm still in shock. I thought he was a prick but now I know he's just a next level piss taker. And he cleans my windows. I love this guy!

━━━━━━━━━━━━━━━━━

Wondering if it's too soon to call Graham.

━━━━━━━━━━━━━━━━━

My car door opened but it was only Judy.

"I'm expecting a package. It should be here around noon. It'll be in your name, but it's for me. I won't be here, I'm meeting someone in the town square. Don't ask any questions and whatever you do, don't open the package. How are the worm farm gags coming along?"

"They're not as interesting as what's going on now."

"I don't trust them…" Judy was talking about the

145

Syrian kids playing in the courtyard next door. She was peering at them in the rear vision mirror.

"They're just kids, Judy."

"We're all just kids, Adam. Now make sure you're here to sign for that package."

And with that Judy hopped out of the car and went back into the house. She's changed. She has a paranoia about her. She's up to something but I can't figure out what.

She yelled from the front door back to the car "… And don't open it!"

Ringer Ringer Ding Dong! Bedford Tennis is about to get a wakeup call. I don't know how it took me this long to figure it out. It's such a simple scam. That I didn't see it straight away is unnerving. I'm losing my edge.

Whenever a new parent brings their kid to the club for a session of tennis, Garry puts an absolute nuff at the other end of the court. It's the same kid every time, the red head who runs like a newborn deer. He always plays just well enough to get the ball back but never good enough to put up a challenge. Throw in the overly positive theatrics of the coach and as a parent you start to think, 'maybe my kid is gifted' and before you know it you've dropped hundreds of pounds into perfecting your child's forehand. But tonight the game changed.

Albie left his coat at the club and old Dad Pants here had to go and get it. And luckily I did, because when I got to the club, what did I see? The red headed nuff absolutely smashing the ball. He made it look effortless, whipping it in from every angle. He had power, finesse, moved like a jungle cat and had an unplayable serve. This kid is an absolute gun, a smoking gun.

It's obvious what's going on. Garry has brought in a Ringer! I see it all. Garry must be paying this kid to throw the practice matches. And this lad is good enough at being bad enough to make your kid look all right. This Ringer is a professional loser and he's been limping around the base line for months, tricking us gullible parents into thinking our children might be special, when in fact, they've always been hopeless. He's the Keyser Soze of tennis! I don't know when and I don't know how, but one day soon Garry and The Ringer will be getting served up some serious comeuppance, Vincent style. That is, in reality, I might make an awkward scene at the tennis club and then go home and tell Lucy what I would have said had I had the courage.

And there it was, a light brown mole to the right of my nose with a dark dot in the middle; I smell melanoma. There is no denying it. Deep down I knew this day was coming. How could it not? Those summer days where I covered myself in oil and fried by the local pool hoping Hayley Nezbit would notice my bronzed biceps; the afternoons I spent at the beach asking the universe to put Hayley Nezbit in a rip tide and allow me to save her; those week long backyard cricket matches I played with my brother all just in case Hayley Nezbit would walk past my front yard, see me take a screamer and then sit on my face; be careful what you wish for.

Australia is the skin cancer capital of the world. You'd be hard pressed to find anyone over sixty who hasn't had a chunk taken out of them at some stage. And they call us, The Lucky Country. Ha! Not if you're the front half of my Uncle Noel's nose. If it was lucky, he'd still have his septum. You can say what you want about Uncle Noel because skin cancer took his ears as well. His face looks like a half-sucked Wot-sit.

I don't want to end up like poor Uncle Noel. If this is cancer, I have to get it early or risk losing everything. Just as I was getting happy too. I've finally made a friend, Lucy is talking to me again, I managed to open up the glove box so now my office has a filing cabinet, plus I've run the sums again and if the kitchen expenses don't blow out too much, I could live comfortably until I'm fifty-nine. But oh no, I have to have a malignant tumour gnawing into my cheekbone. Seeing a doctor is nearly impossible too, the average waiting time is three weeks! Three long weeks. It could be in my lungs by then. What annoys me is if one of my kids get sick, they get seen almost straight away. Don't get me wrong, when your child is ill, you're grateful to be seen that day, but what about the hard working father? Kids don't pay tax. I'm the one helping pay the doctors wages. They need to keep me on the pitch, not an eight-year-old who can scratch himself in the morning and be fully healed by lunch. I've got skin cancer! I could be dead in two weeks.

I called at eight a.m., immediately I was put on hold. Ten minutes later, I finally get through, I tell the receptionist I'm from Australia, that a childhood crush kept me in the sun too long, that Mount Rushmore is carving itself out of my face. I really sold it, almost cried and what do I get in return? A three and a half week wait time.

"Three and a half weeks? I'll be dead by then," I said. The receptionist called my bluff. "If you think you're close to dying you should go to accident and emergency." I can't go to A&E with a melanoma, they'll laugh at me. I'd rather die.

New business idea:

If the NHS are going to offer kids 'same day' appointments, then surely I can use it to my advantage?

My initial thought was 'why don't I start giving Albie my symptoms?' But that's too short sited. Why stop with just my symptoms? Why not build a market where people start paying for Albie to act as a proxy for their illness? If Garry Foxe can profit from using a Ringer, then I could use Albie to help speed things up with the local doctors.

I'll have to teach him how to act and cut him in on some the profits, but this could be a great little side hustle. It's so clear in my mind.

"OK, son, here's a list of today's ailments: Firstly, Bob's gout has flared up again. He tells me he's hobbling around like a leper in a mouse trap factory and is fresh out of ideas on what to do. He'll give you twenty quid if you can convince the doctor that you have gout and another forty if you can come back with a remedy. Next up we have Kevin, he can't stop crying and wonders what he's done with his life. We all know the answer but sometimes you have to hear it from a professional. You're only ten so it's a tricky sell but if you could get the doctor to prescribe you something to help take the edge off the anxiety, Kevin is offering us another fifty quid. Next on the list is me. You might not want to hear this but it hurts when I pee. Not all the time but when it does happen I get a sharp pain right up in my dot. If you could pass that onto the doctor I'll sling you another ten."

"Dad, I'm worried about you."

"Me? I'm fine! You're the one with all the

problems. All you have to do is sell them."

Lucy thinks I'm an idiot and Judy threatened to call social services, so my plan may have to sit on the back burner, but I reckon it's got legs. I could train a load of kids to feign illness. Note to self: work on pitch for Dragon's Den.

Lucy and Judy stood in the shell of the new room, where the old perfectly workable kitchen used to be, chatting to Steve the builder. His cohort of tradesman were busy loading up drills and power sanders and nail guns and angle grinders and electric saws and what looked like about eighty different types of screwdriver, into their respective boxes. I lurked in the background hoping someone would inform me on the room's progress. Builders never speak to me, it's always Lucy. Even when she isn't around and they need approval on a new expense or where to put what, they'll call out to her, never me, ever.

Last week Lucy went out for the day. Everyone was informed of her absence. Her last words to the builders were 'if you need anything just call out to Adam'. It's not a hard name to remember, according to the bible I was the first one here. But no, I spent the day sat in the lounge room, waiting for the inevitable call only for some bloke to scream, 'Lucy!'

"My name is Adam! I'm paying for it! The least you can do is learn my name!" I said with a decreasing volume to avoid actual conflict.

"Sorry... Adam... we just want to know where exactly do you want your down lights positioned?"

"Down lights... yes... exactly... I'll have to call Lucy."

And that was the last time I was referred to by my name.

So, this afternoon with Lucy back on deck I stood back hoping to get an idea on when these very well paid men would be vamoosing from my life.

"...The steels are in, they took some negotiating, mainly with Al's big hammer but we got there, didn't we Al?"

"My hammer can be very persuasive," Al said, like the Cheeky Chappy he no doubt is.

Well, with that Judy started chuckling under her breath like a giddy school girl and then it developed into full blown hysterics and she had to leave the room.

"Sorry, my mother hasn't seen a persuasive hammer in a very long time and she also has a mind that belongs in the gutter," Lucy said trying to save the day.

Everyone was laughing now. Poor Al became very red faced and went back to packing up his big hammers. Judy's laugh carried through the house and up the stairs. Her giggle is infectious.

"So when do you think we'll get our lives back?" I asked wanting to hear 'next week' or 'not long now' but mainly to stop any more talk about Al's big hammer.

"Another three weeks, maybe four," Steve said.

"Three or four weeks! That's a lot of stew!"

Knowing we'd be down a stove Lucy went out and dropped twenty quid on a slow cooker and we've been eating stews ever since. Nothing good comes from casserole.

Completely oblivious, Steve then casually mentioned, "There is an issue of rising damp."

"That sounds expensive," I said hoping I was wrong.

"It's just in your back corner, you can see it here…"

Steve pointed to a damp patch of wall where our fridge used to live.

"It certainly looks damp but are you sure it's rising?" I said in my manliest of manly voices hoping I'd come across like someone who couldn't be swindled.

Rising damp is ripe for the swindle. By design it's meant to sound ominous. You're left wondering, how far does it rise? Where will it rise to? Will it give my children mouldy lung? Is this all just a giant con to rinse me for more money half-way through a build when you know I'd happily walk across hot coals if it meant you leaving my house?

Steve played us beautifully.

"It's definitely damp and it's definitely rising. Look to be honest you really want it out of the house, especially with the kids. Hopefully it'll only set you back a few hundred but trust me, it's the best option."

"Just put it on the tab, we'll be right," I said patting Lucy on the shoulder. If I was going to get shafted, I wanted her to at least think it was my decision.

"Well, thanks for all your work guys I'll be in my office as I have an important deadline that can't be moved. If you see a hose funnelled into the car window don't try and stop me!"

Everyone laughed, everyone but me.

Graham arrived with another thermos. This time it contained a smidge of gin. Don't mind if I do.

He totally agrees with me on my face mole.

"You lucky bastard! You'll be out of here in a few months. No more bills, no more getting upset that you've never achieved anything. Albie won't mind calling me dad, will he?"

"I see you've taken your arsehole pills this morning."

"That's it, get it all out," laughed Graham, "if you hold those feelings in it'll only spread the cancer faster."

We ran off and refilled that thermos three times. Again, I'm flirting with that weird emotion they call happiness.

Glen wants me in the studio all next week which means I have to schlep it into London during peak hour paying full whack on my ticket, all so I can hear Francis bang on about banging on. He's probably had an affair with a Russian spy or eaten caviar out of a ballerina's arsehole or opened up a breakfast bar in Fulham that has swapped plates for seventies style ashtrays. I refuse to get depressed about it. If there's one thing the last few weeks have taught me it's that you can be positive about having a shit life.

I Love Bedford! I love Bedford! I Love Bedford! Bedford! Bedford! Bedford! Love! Love! Love!

Maybe my daily mantra is working? Lately my life has been full of adventure. How many comedians get to write jokes for late night infomercials? Most of them would sell their mother for late night infomercial money. I'm making two thousand pounds next week. Two thousand pounds! That's exciting, plus I can tell Francis that I DJ'd a giraffe to the point of collapse.

━━━━━━━━━━━━━━━━━━━━━━━━━━

Today was an absolute stinker.

The train was late to arrive, then its departure was delayed, then it was held between Harpenden and St Albans, then it was hit by an out of this world funk that wafted through three carriages and into the souls of all who dared sniff it.

I don't know who it was, or what they ate but if you

boiled a bag of skunks and strained their gelatinous goop through a homeless guy's underpants and buried any leftover sediment in wet dog shit, that smell would be friendlier than the odour which punched my nostrils this morning. It was chunky. The stench only got worse when the train was held fifty metres from St. Pancras station because of a man on the tracks. I imagine the poor soul wanted to end it because he got whiff of what was happening on our carriage. People were doing all they could to cover their nose, using jumpers, rolling deodorant on sleeves, stuffing newspapers up their snouts, it was horrific. Whatever the reason, it was a nasty way to start my latest contract. I walked into the office forty minutes late and smelling nastier than a dead goat.

To call it an office was a stretch. It was more a sub-let office inside a bigger office that was full of empty coat racks. It was a cloak room. Three floors up, and the only window looked out onto bricks. The desk they'd provided was more a bench that could barely seat four but for some reason came with eight chairs. Francis, and his lanky frame, took up half of the space. He sat there like we'd just leased the top floor of The Shard. Leaning back with his skinny-jean-wearing legs flopped over the table, his ankles showing off those low-cut socks that don't want to be socks. His arms were folded behind his head making him look completely relaxed, without a worry in the world, until you got to his mouth which was, as per, enthusiastically chewing gum. This was a ploy he used to convince people he was a deep thinker, a mover and a shaker, a prick. Glen stood on the other side of the room like a faded eighties rockstar, ragged, well past his prime, probably drunk, but clearly the only reason either Francis or I were there.

"Fuck'n shit, open up the window. Fuck'n crikey! You brought in a wicked fuck'n pong with ya this morning, mate. Stone the fuck'n crows!"

"Sorry, it wasn't originally my smell, it came from the train but it must've migrated."

"It is rather offensive…" Francis said, pulling his T-shirt over his nose before opening up the window.

"Thanks, Francis. Right, yes, I stink and I'm late. My apologies, it's been a shit morning."

"Smells like you've been fuck'n rolling in it… Francis, hurry up and let's get this done." Glen and Francis put their noses either side of the window and took in some deep breaths. They couldn't look at me.

"Sorry, Adam, I was out till three last night, dinner and drinks with the lads at The Phene Bar in Chelsea. That smell is playing havoc with my hangover. Okay, so we need half a day of writing on stainless carpet, samples will be dropped off here at eleven but the premise is straight forward, it's carpet that can't be stained. We'll need enough material to carry Glen for twenty minutes. It's one of our biggest contracts yet so make it fun and they love anything physical. You'll have loads of room to move, so Glen, feel free to get crazy."

"We're on Friday night at eleven! I'll be going properly fuck'n troppo don't you worry about that." Glen punched the air adding to his eighties persona before re-sniffing the room and returning his nose to the fresher scents of London. The city smelled better than I did. Ouch.

"Go team," I said, hoping my positivity would shift the focus.

"It is very good, Glen, the channel are super impressed, you're getting a cult-like following. The online traction alone is keeping the clients more than happy. You've got over ten thousand twitter followers. Adam, might be good if you could write up some tweets."

"Sure," I quipped, like it was nothing, but I was definitely going to be asking for more money.

"*Righto*, as you Aussies like to say. Adam, after this morning's writing session, you'll be heading over to the Riverside Studios in Hammersmith to meet Glen for the Worm Farm record. The clients have approved the scripts but would like us to try and sell the eco-friendly aspect of the worms as it will play well to the hipsters. They'd love it if you could make that work."

"Piece of piss," I said, matching Australianisms with Glen.

"Brilliant. Glen, am I right in thinking for the rest of the week you and Adam will be meeting up here and working on this Friday's record?"

"You've fuck'n nailed it. Works for you, doesn't it,

cunt?" Glen asked the question knowing I had no real choice in the answer.

I played along for the money, "No wucken furries!"

Glen clapped his hands in triumph and made to leave.

"Brilliant! Righto, I'm off to speak to the sales team about what else is in the pipeline for Friday's record. I've told them I only sell products I believe in. Last week they suggested I flog fuck'n spandex pants. Me? Spandex? These pricks have no idea. Anyway, I'll see you there at three. Adam, maybe at lunch try and buy a new shirt or one of those scented fuck'n trees to wrap around your neck. I'm trying to tune one of the runners and your stench will do me no favours. Later, cunts."

And then, he was gone. I still had loads of unanswered questions. Questions like: why did I spend ninety minutes on a train for a meeting that could have easily been done over Zoom? Or... How did Glen get a cult following when he acts like a total spanner? Maybe... Am I the punchline of a TV prank that involves Glen convincing a desperate comedian he can get paid to write jokes about stainless carpet? It hurts me knowing I'll never get an answer to any of these questions.

Once Glen had departed it was just Francis and I sitting together, him desperately wanting to leave and escape my waft and me realising I could have some fun.

"How was your weekend, Francis?"

"'Um, well, I'll have to tell you tomorrow as I'm

due in a meeting with the channel at ten, but trust me when I say it was… good."

"Only 'good'? How boring, I killed a giraffe."

"Brilliant! Brilliant! I have to dash." And with that Francis tucked his nose back into his expensive T-shirt and headed out the door.

And then I was left alone. I immediately launched into a fifteen minute power nap that lasted an hour before racing off to Hammersmith to make TV.

I say TV. Really, I spent the afternoon watching Glen tell the world he had worms. He dragged his arse across the studio floor, rubbed his gums with fresh worm droppings, and stapled himself with food scraps while being lowered into a bath full of compost. Part Steve Irwin part Mr Tumble, Glen was incredible to watch. There was nobody who could out-dickhead Glen.

We finished around six and then I set off home.

I got in at nine o'clock to hear Lucy and her mum laughing. Exhausted but happy, I felt as if I'd actually achieved something even though I hadn't really done anything.

It's amazing how working with Glen and hearing about all the times he nearly married a prostitute can make you forget you have face cancer. For the last two days I had completely forgotten that I could be dying. But tonight,

I stared deep into the bathroom mirror and was reminded that my life might soon be over and if that's the case, then thus far my life's work, my magnum opus, is suggesting to an unhinged Australian that he pretend to have an itchy arse. I have more to give.

━━━━━━━━━━━━━━━━━━━━━━━━━━━━━

Another day, another chance to write jokes about a product I can't imagine people buying. Glen and I strapped on our abs belts hoping to get a feel for where the jokes might be. With our shirts-off we sat in the office, and let the machine work its magic on our guts. Surely the laughs were in how we looked? Glen's paunch flapped over his belt, mine was just as unflattering. It was a laugh or cry situation. I chose laughter but a few moments in and Glen burst into tears. The machine must have hit a nerve because he completely lost it. He was bawling. He hasn't seen his kids in eight months, his ex-wife has taken off with a welder from Leeds, he's on the cock pills because the booze has left him impotent. And the biggest bombshell of them all, "I'm not even Australian, mate! I was born in Margate. Dad moved us to Perth for a job when I was fifteen. I spent the first five years getting picked on for being a Pom. I learnt how to speak Australian watching the Mad Max series. I'm a fuck'n fraud, Adam! I've been telling people for years that I couldn't give a brass razoo but I have no idea what a brass razoo is."

"Don't worry, no one does, mate."

All while our abs burred in the background. Maybe his stomach muscles being worked over made him face some home truths. Not sure.

"I'm a sad sack of fuck'n shit!"

"Nah you're not, mate, your fans love you, you're on the cusp of infomercial brilliance and besides, five years living in Perth is twenty Australian years everywhere else. You're a fully-fledged Aussie, mate!"

"You sure, mate?"

"Mate, you're a fair dinkum Aussie, you fuck dingos for Christ's sake and I don't even know what that means."

"Thanks, mate!"

"No worries, cobber."

It was a strange day.

Got home at seven, showered, hopped into the car for a gig in Kettering. They frowned through the Tomato gear but enjoyed the new stuff on Doctors, plus I made two hundred pounds, bonza!

I've come to love walking home from the train, and standing on the other side of the street watching my family go about their business. I'll see Albie disturbing Lizzie downstairs in the front room, trying to get her to take the bait. Lucy will be there sorting through school bags looking for jumpers and homework knowing exactly when to break up the kid's, inevitable, cushion fight. Judy is always up in her loft headfirst into her computer, probably ordering another mysterious box from Amazon. It's been a parcel a day from her lately. Watching my family going through their nightly rituals brings me calm, but I know as soon as I walk through the front door, they will all do my head in. We drive each other nuts. They'll scream about this and I'll yell about that, and then one of us will cry and it'll be me who is blamed. Before I've been given a fair hearing the family will decide that, again, I'm the grumpy bastard. I know this. The perfect option would be to move in across the street and just watch them from a safe distance.

Tonight, I walked in angry. I stood out the front and saw a full skip spewing dust and grit onto the windscreen of my Hyundai office. I saw polystyrene packaging, hopefully from our new fridge, scattered across the front of the garden but most shockingly I noticed that one of the windows had been boarded up with a piece of ply. Instead of viewing the normal family chaos all I could see was an expensive mess.

I walked in the door and tried to contain my grumpy bastard face, "Who broke the high-end sash window?" Not a great start.

"It was an accident. Steve was kind enough to put up some board." Lucy was bathing Lizzie upstairs. The old hide behind the fact you're a good mother trick. Clever.

"He's paying for it. They break it; they fix it."

"Adam, you don't know what you're talking about. Just give me two minutes to sort the kids." She stared down at me from the landing rubbing Lizzie's head furiously with a towel.

"Ouch!" Lizzie wasn't wrapped with her technique.

"That'll cost hundreds of pounds. I basically went to work for nothing. I would have been better off..."

"...staying at home and guarding the house." Lucy knew me well.

"It was the Arabs," Judy called down from her room. Three floors, three opinions.

"Who are the Arabs?" I had to know.

"Next doors lot, you won't let me call them Gypsies, but they're your culprits. They're vile, the lot of them." Is there any point trying to change an old lady's attitude to brown people?

"What are Arabs?" Albie yelled from his room.

"Mum, they're not vile..." (to Albie)... "they are Syrian refugees, they had to escape their country and found safety in ours."

"Hi, Dad," said Albie.

"Hi Big Man. So, it wasn't the builders? How did next door's lot break my window?" I asked the house.

"Your window? Ha!" Judy had come down from her cave and was now helping Albie find his pyjamas.

"The kids next door were playing football and one

164

of them kicked the ball into the window. The dad came over with his little boy and made him apologise. The poor guy looked so sorry and sad and so tired. His poor teeth were rotten. I told him…"

"… That it was fine and not to worry about it." I could finish Lucy's sentences just as well as she could finish mine. Why did I marry a do-gooder? She's so easily manipulated.

"The small kid next door? Kicked the ball into our window?"

"Yes. He apologised, we'll pay for it, it will be fine."

"But that kid is so tiny."

"Adam, leave it." Lucy was in no mood but how could I let it go? It was obvious that her story made no sense.

As you look at our house, to our left we have the exceptionally loving couple we share the semi with and to our right you have a courtyard followed by a group of flats.

The Syrians are a married couple with a teenage boy and a young tot who couldn't have been more than five years old and two feet tall. I know this because we'd already had a run in. Last Sunday they used the courtyard as a football pitch and the side of our house as the goal. There's not much worse than having a ball kicked against your wall. Aside from maybe being petrol bombed by Assad. I could hear them laughing as they played, perhaps for the first time in years, but the issue was, I was trying to nap. You have to set the precedent quickly in these situations. I can't let them bang away and then come out a month later and put a stop to it. You have to rule your end-of-terrace wall with an iron fist. So out I went ready to be friendly but firm. Given what they've been through I probably shouldn't have shook my fist and yelled, 'this is my wall'. But does that justify them breaking my window and then lying about it? And there can be no doubt, they were lying. The evidence was in the maths.

Before the ball can get to my side window it has to be kicked over a brick wall that is six feet high. To do this you would have to have a reasonable boot on you. In my estimations, combining Pythagoras' theorem of C squared equals A squared plus B squared with Einstein's E equals M C squared, to get the correct amount of E to cover the distance of C you would have to be at least fourteen years old! You definitely couldn't be a small child like the one that Lucy claims apologised. A kid who is only two foot tall does not have the oomph in his foot to clear the distance. So, therefore, I can only deduce that the father from next door got his younger kid to apologise knowing full well that it was the older kid who did the kicking. Lee Harvey Oswald didn't shoot Kennedy just like that little Syrian boy didn't break my window. It was his brother or even worse, a mystery kicker from the other side of the street. Either way the little boy was being used to cover up the crime.

Lucy wasn't convinced. We argued our way to the temporary kitchen. No cooking was involved but pots were being stirred.

"So, you're saying Omar lied?" Great, she was already on a first named basis with the guy. I mean brilliant and beautiful and generous but not helping my cause.

"There's no way that little tacker made that kick honey, it's too far and his legs are too small?"

"Shall I call the police?" Judy was way too keen.

"He had rotten teeth, he was tired. Ali is just sixteen and looks shell-shocked and little Latif is so cute. They just escaped a war-torn country! We have the money," said Lucy having temporarily forgotten our financial situation.

"It's the principle darling, the man lied." Judy with the counter punch.

"We're not charging them for the window. End of..." Lucy stormed off upstairs to do some angry clothes folding while the kids ran into their rooms keen to avoid any crossfire. Angry clothes folding was Lucy's final warning. The cracking sounds of T-shirts and trousers fresh off the clothes horse were tell-tale signs that the argument would go no further. One night I got on the wrong side of tipsy in London and slept through my train stop, ending up in Wellingborough and didn't get back until six a.m. I woke up to see ironed socks on my pillow which is the linen equivalent of waking up to see a horse's head.

Judy dashed upstairs, "I'm going to give the kids a walkie talkie so they can call me if they see something suspicious. You can't be too careful." Judy was off the charts ridiculous.

"Good idea, Judy, get the kids scared of the neighbours before bed," I shouted, knowing I had no power to stop her crazy antics etching themselves into my children's consciousness. But who was I to take that memory from them?

So, again, I'm left alone in the lounge room, this time staring at a freshly boarded up window. There would be no hot dinner, no 'how was your day?' Just the usual guilty feeling that I was the one causing all the trouble.

Not that my argument wasn't irrefutable. It will all go down on Saturday. They'll see. I'll see to it that they'll see.

I need to go to bed.

———————————————————

Last night's shoot rolled on until 1 a.m. We shot three products over six hours. Stainless carpet, an electronic abs machine and spandex pants for men. Even Glen had a price. He looked hilarious in spandex, like a before and after picture except his after was more 'after a good Christmas'.

I could study Glen for years. He's a complete car

crash of a man but he oozes charisma. The lovable rogue who got a taste for blagging his way through life and now can't stop himself. He left a message on my phone this morning and sounded like he'd spent all night on the gack.

"Mate, my fuck'n twitter notifications are on fire… not as much as that flam'n carpet was last night, didn't that fucker light up? Fuck a duck, I thought I was hav'n a fuck'n stroke, but it was the bloody shag pile. The shit they must spray on that to make it stain free. Don't worry, legal reckons they can't touch us. Anyway, well done, son, you make me look good, more on the way in a month or two I promise. Later, cunt!"

It seems under the heat of studio lights stainless carpet is flammable which was funny at the time but in the cold light of day feels ethically dubious. I'll take the money but avoid the product. A month or two before another contract is too long away from infomercial money. I've got three or four gigs lined up but after those the diary is dry. I was hoping Glen would land another contract this week. I need the money. Not that it's his fault my window has been kicked in or that Steve found rising damp in one of the walls. Four hundred pounds he quoted! I spat my tea onto the kitchen floor when Lucy told me which only added to the problem. Four hundred pounds for damp! If energy costs were friendlier I'd sneak a studio light into my house and sort the problem myself.

After knocking for several minutes, I was finally greeted at the door by Omar, the lying father. Lucy was right, his teeth were shocking and he did look tired. Omar's youngest son, Latif, clung to his leg while the older more sheepish looking son, Ali, stood behind them unwilling to catch my eye.

I went in strong, "Hello, you know who I am don't you? The bloke from next door…"

They smiled and nodded but offered little in the way of a 'hello' back.

"… Yes, you know who I am. Right, two days ago you spoke to Lucy, my lovely but easily manipulated wife."

I lowered my voice remembering that not having a decent grasp of English didn't mean you were deaf.

"Lucy tells me your little fella here kicked his football over that wall…"

I pointed back at the wall and struggled to hide my utter disbelief.

"And the ball broke our window. Yes?"

Omar's tired smile was replaced with concern.

"Lucy also tells me she said we'd pay for all the damage. Isn't that lovely? I just came over to say it's OK don't worry about it. We will do just that, we will pay for the window."

I stood at the front of their ground floor flat wanting at minimum a 'thank-you' but was aiming for an admission of guilt.

"It's quite the kick, isn't it? That must be what? Twenty feet? The fence is at least six feet high. You can't be more than what? Four? That's a big kick for such a small little boy. You sure it wasn't your older brother back there? The one who won't look me in the eye? Dad, what do you reckon?"

Omar stood unmoved in the doorway. If he didn't understand my words, he definitely understood my tone. So, I kept going.

"Look, we all know what's going on here. I just wanted to say we're happy to pay for the window, it's fine, Lucy tells me you escaped from Syria. I am also a refugee. I came from Australia where it's beautiful. We're not that different, none of us want to be in Bedford. We're all a bit shell shocked, you probably more than me, that's a given. But with regards to the window, no hard feelings."

I then slowly walked back from their door waiting for any hint of a thank-you or smidge of gratitude, any tiny tinge of a 'sorry' but my words had gone for nothing. I couldn't believe it. I marched back to their door, crouched down and spoke to the little boy.

"I will give you forty quid if you make that shot again. Forty! Fair? Forty quid?" Sensing danger Omar picked up Latif while Ali whispered something in his ear. He suddenly seemed much more engaged.

171

"Oh, now your eyes light up, when you see the big bills come out."

I put my hand into my pocket and pulled out the cash to prove I wasn't mucking around.

"There you go forty of this country's finest. All you have to do, son, is kick that ball over the wall and back into my window and I'll give you the money. And if you miss, well that's fine too, you owe me nothing, except maybe, an apology…"

Omar turned to his son, Ali, and chatted away in their mother tongue. I knew I'd struck a chord as they were getting very animated.

"I bet you're discussing how you get out of this one. This is what happens when you try and play me for a mug!"

Then Ali piped up, "Fifty-quid?"

I couldn't believe it, "Fifty? Make it seventy! No, one hundred! I will give you guys one hundred pounds if your little brother can defy basic physics and kick that ball back into my window."

Another small conference and then Ali put his hand out and we shook on it. It was happening.

Word spread from house to house and it wasn't too long before a small crowd had formed along the street. Gina looked down from her balcony, Graham pulled up a deck chair, Lucy, Judy and the kids watched on. Kevin was there although he was quickly called back in by Sylvia. Steve and his builder mates, who should've been working double time to finish the damn kitchen, took their lunch break early to see if the boy had what it took.

"Twenty on the boy!" shouted Gina.

"Same!" yelled Graham.

"Surely you're on my side, mate?"

"I am, Adam, this is just dickhead insurance."

"Fifty says the boy won't make it," said Judy who looked very sure of herself. Finally, we agreed on something.

"Fifty says he does." Not afraid to divide the house Lucy was firmly behind the boy.

The builders started placing bets amongst themselves, and Ali was playing the role of bookie, running around collecting cash and IOU's, the courtyard was in a frenzy. An Amazon delivery guy pulled over to see what the fuss was, he wound down his window and put a fiver on the kid.

"OK, all bets are closed. Here are the rules. If the lad here can kick his ball into my window, sorry, back… into my window, then I give him one hundred pounds. If he can't, both he and his father owe me an apology. Hands have been shaken, the deal is done. Let's go!"

Latif looked nervous as he put the ball into position. He turned to Omar seeking his confidence. Omar nodded stoically. If ever there was a face that said, 'kick away my son' it was Omar's. I was beaming. This was a sure thing. Twenty-feet-long, six-feet-high, never.

Silence fell. The boy was on his toes, ready to come in for the kick. One step, two steps, a third then whack! The ball flew through the air, it was an almighty kick, the crowd rose as one, arms were outstretched, faces were jubilant, could it be happening? Was the world ready for what this kid was kicking? No. The ball crashed into the wall. I turned to face Omar.

"I told you! Did I not tell you? Yes!"

I pumped my fists in the air like I had just won the World Cup for Australia. I couldn't contain my joy. Finally, I'd had a win. Unfortunately, half way through attempting the caterpillar I noticed the ball had rebounded off the wall and was flying back towards Latif with force. He kicked it again but it was a bigger kick than before, one that leveraged the momentum, returning it through the air with interest. While I was jumping around like an idiot the ball fizzed over the fence, heading higher than anyone would've thought possible and quickly smashing through the window above the one that had already been broken. My triumph turned into shock and the crowd's disappointment turned into a raucous celebration. What rotten luck.

Now I'm down a hundred pounds and two windows need replacing. It's a disaster. Lucy apologised to Omar. Before heading inside, she kissed me on the cheek, "You are a first rate plonker." She's right. I am a dickhead. I never even considered the power of the bounce back. What a fool!

"We are going to talk about this for years," said Graham as he laughed himself home. Eventually it was just me Omar and his boys. I handed over what money I had.

"I owe you all an apology. That's quite a boot you have on you, little man. I'm sorry I assumed you were lying. I'll head off now to get the rest."

Omar spoke to Ali who then spoke to me, "Can we get it in twenties?"

"Yep," I said defeated.

"And can we get the ball back?"

"Yep, that too."

And as the courtyard cleared and the workmen started knocking up another sheet of plywood to fix another hole in my house, I opened my office door, sat down and head butted the steering wheel until the pain went away.

Finally got to see my doctor. Not that he's my doctor. I have no idea who 'my 'doctor is. I simply sit down in the waiting area and wait for my name to be called over the crackly tannoy.

"Adam to see Dr Fixa – (crackle crackle), big – (static screeching sound), gibbons (whistling noise that makes the deaf guy next to me check his hearing aid)."

I think she said, Dr Fixabiggibbons? I'd never heard of this person before in my life. I walked up a set of rickety stairs turned left and was confronted by two nameless doors. Which door do I choose? Can't they at least come out and greet me with a 'hello'? What if I accidentally walk in on a prostate check? Or someone being told they have cancer? And we wonder why anxiety disorders are sky high. Luckily, I heard a door open and a voice call my name. I was up another floor.

Dr Fixabiggibbons was actually called, Dr Gibbons. A plump and serious looking man with rhubarb red skin. A wheeze emanated from his chest which made him look as though he was mid heart attack. Why is it I'm yet to meet a healthy doctor? It's disconcerting. Do all the doctors look tired and puffy in the face? I think Dr Gibbons tactic was to make the patient feel better just by looking worse. You'd limp in with a sore foot and skip out thinking, 'at least I'm not *that* guy'. It's a worrying indictment on our health system that Dr Gibbons has access to all the pills, yet he still looks like shit.

Prescribe yourself something, mate!

Of course, I didn't say any of this because I'd never met the man before which, when you think about it, is ridiculous. Our builder, Steve, came highly recommended and he even showed us his previous work. My mechanic, Darrel up the road, had good word of mouth so now I let him fix my busted up Hyundai. Lucy and I tried twelve kinds of pillow until we found one that did the job (Hungarian Goose Down, thoroughly recommend). But when my life is at stake what am I doing? I'm putting my trust in the hands of some joker I've never met before. What a system! What an idiot! I was giving this fat mess of a man cart-blanche to oversee my health and ultimately my family's financial security. My mouth said, "Hello." But my mind said, "Run!"

"So, Mr Vincent, what seems to be the problem?"

"I have a spot on my face that has recently appeared, it's brown and I suspect it's cancer…"

Lots of wheezing, lots of coughing but no actual response which only made me talk more. I told this cream-puff of a man about my history of growing up in a country that was located under a magnifying glass. I told him about Uncle Noel's chewed on head and why I believed Halloween has no place in Australian culture. It all went for zip. I quickly deduced that Mr Gibbons had the communication skills of a toddler wearing a mouth guard. I spilled my guts and he sat there wheezing away before turning to his computer. I assumed it was to look up my medical history but that would require common sense. Instead, I noticed that Dr Gibbons was google imaging melanoma!

I had been doing that for weeks!

I was three feet away from this wheezing walrus, hardly close enough for him to have a thorough examination but he looked at his screen and then looked at me, then back to the screen. I had to move my chair closer to him and point out my own potential death spot. "I think you need to really see it don't you?" His next move was an absolute fucking doozy. Dr Gibbons took off his glasses and wiped them with his shirt before wincing and telling me that, "It will probably be all right."

"Excuse me?"

"It doesn't look like anything to me. It will probably be all right."

Wincing? Probably? 'Probably be all right' is not what you want to hear when you think you have face cancer. 'Probably be all right' is what you say when you park your car a little bit over the line. Or when your three-year-old punches themselves in the face whenever they see the colour yellow. I was pretty sure it was probably cancer. I asked if we could get a second opinion and Dr Gibbons looked around his otherwise empty room and said, "I don't think so." Then he wheezed into his hanky and steered me to the door. I was so stunned by his complete lack of everything, that I did what he said.

I don't know what I was hoping for but it wasn't a wince and it definitely wasn't a 'probably be all right'.

In hindsight what I really wanted was confidence. I wanted Dr Gibbons to look at my face and then get on the intercom to the receptionist.

"Doreen can you whip up a lolly pop for this prick who thinks he has cancer please? It's a freckle at best son, now stop wasting taxpayers money and get out of my office."

A forthright 'fuck off' would've served me much better than a wheezy wincy maybe way-be 'probably be all right'.

"Harry, I'm worried I might have skin cancer…"

"That's unlucky?"

"Any tips on how to deal with the anxiety of a positive diagnosis?"

"Oh, mate, you just crack on, try to have a laugh and make the most of what time you have left," said Harry without the slightest tinge of sadness in his voice.

"It's not definite that I have cancer, the doctor reckons I needn't worry. Should I?"

"Yeah you should always get a second opinion. It took me six doctors until I found one who believed me!"

"Really? Six doctors?"

"It took me years to find the right specialist. It was horrible. But nothing beats the certainty of knowing it's all over."

"How have you coped for this long?"

"You push on, Adam, you push on, speaking of which do you want a gig in Bath next Tuesday? If they like you it could lead to more work."

"Sure, Harry."

Harry. The best-worst agent in the business who almost definitely doesn't have cancer.

Had my first proper deep and meaningful with Graham. We were on our now semi-regular walk around the river.

179

Our aim is to get fit while looking ridiculous and our motto is 'full kit, long strides'. Today I got us wearing headbands for the laugh. Little did I know.

"…So that's why I think he's a crook," I said having spent the last five hundred yards detailing the darker side of Garry Foxe. "What about you? What's happening in your world?"

"Well, we've extended the mortgage and we're flying out later this week for ten days in Arizona," said Graham, stopping for the lights and checking his pulse.

"Arizona! What? Why? I thought you couldn't afford holidays because you were on a four day week?"

"We can't afford it but my marriage is on its knees. We're desperate for a break and Jess has always wanted to see the Grand Canyon, so her mum is taking the kids and we're off. One hundred and thirty beats a minute. Not bad."

"When?" I asked, now counting my pulse.

"Next week."

"Next week! But what about our walk? One hundred and ten, too low."

"We'll have other walks," cried Graham.

"You know what this means?"

"What?"

"Lucy is going to want a holiday!"

"What rubbish," Graham said turning to face me. "You always make her sound so shallow, Adam, and she's not, you've got a wonderful wife."

"I know that," I said doing my best to combine

looking concerned with jogging on the spot.

"Do you though? Do you really? Because I thought I had a wonderful wife but two nights ago, Jess had her bags packed and not for a trip to Arizona." Graham, looked as serious as one can get in a light blue tracksuit with mismatching headband.

"I'm sorry, mate, I had no idea. You're always so happy, even when you're down, you're up," I said, bringing my on the spot jog to a halt.

"Well, for the record, I'm down," Graham sighed almost on the verge of tears. "I'm sorry for getting cranky but I nearly lost her, Adam. Had the Wi-Fi dropped off and I'd not been able to book flights then and there, she would've walked."

"The area has had rubbish internet lately."

"My heart was in my mouth the entire time. At one point I got rainbow and thought it was over. I was a mess."

"So you guys are OK now?" I asked as we both restarted our walk.

"Just, it's costing me five nights at an All Inclusive and I have to spend three days on the back of a horse but if my marriage needs a holiday to survive then that is what I'll give it."

"Fair enough."

"It is fair enough. I'm baking pies, you're creating drama wherever you can, our struggles are obvious but, Jess, she's kept it all in and suddenly she's at the pack your bags stage of what I hope is only a rough patch in our marriage."

"I'm sorry, mate," I said, and I was. We both stood there, in our three stripe tracksuits, hugging it out at the traffic lights.

"Me too. All we can do is move forward."

And we did.

"I don't create drama, do I?"

"You made us wear headbands, Adam."

It all started so well.

We set off for a picnic at Wrest Park. It was to be our first ever No Screen Sunday. Lucy's idea. No Netflix, no Twitter, no phones! But lots of feeling that we were better than everyone else for doing it.

With a Grade 1 heritage listing and fields for miles Wrest Park is the perfect place to feel the smugness that comes from being a non-screening bastard. You can lose yourself in the hoity-toity gardens but more importantly, you can lose your children. The kids can run off to find frogs and pick wild flowers and make as much noise as they like without getting the usual screams of 'quiet down' from me. Once or twice I fulfilled my fatherly obligations and chased them through the trees but most of my time was spent with Lucy. The two of us had great fun pretending we were aristocrats taking a turn around the gardens, planning our next soiree.

"Shall we have the Cavendishes over for dinner next week?"

"Indeed, we shall."

"We'll have to head out on a hunt, we're all out of pheasant and deer."

"Indeed, tell me, how are we for virgins? The last one we sacrificed lacked purity. Why, I drank her blood and believe I actually aged."

"Yes, sorry about that, we found out she wasn't a virgin at all, but liked to play the flute behind the orangery."

"The flute you say? How sordid, well we can't be having that."

"Quite."

"Quite."

Meanwhile Judy was off, walking around the manor house reliving past glories.

"I do love the Rococo period? Everything was just so marvellous!"

As a rule, Judy found any heritage listed building we visited to be 'marvellous'. The way she announced the word 'marvellous' was extraordinary. Her head would reach for the clouds, her chest would heave on the in-breath and out the word would boom, 'Maaar-vellous,'; she said it in a whip like fashion. The 'Mar ' would take an age while the remaining syllables 'vel' and 'lous' were snapped in before anyone knew what was going on. It was a sight and sound to behold. Like a posh baby penguin on a cliff edge calling for her mother to come back from the ocean and feed her more herring. They say never forget where you came from and you couldn't fault Judy on this. She walked around Wrest Park like she owned the joint and if you believed her stories, there was a world where she once could have owned the lot. In her own way she'd had a tough life. From almost touching aristocracy to living on the top floor of a semidetached house in Bedford is quite the fall. But say what you like about Judy, and I often do, she always carries herself with exuberance and grace and my children adore her for it, especially on days like today. She charges with them through the trees hunting the imaginary trolls that kidnapped the princess. When I hear her wicked and raucous laugh melding with their shrieks of excitement it's hard not to love the lady. She may think that I'm a failure but she loves my children and they love her and when combined with a sunny day, that is enough.

It really was a great afternoon. One of our best in a while.

On the way home the kids sat in the back seat with Judy, all three scoffing down their ice creams. Lucy put on the radio and popped her hand on my knee. Queen's We Are The Champions, came on and we all started singing and giggling. I even landed a parking space right out the front of our house. The drive back was indeed, marvellous.

Unfortunately, as I walked up to the house I looked through the window and noticed that the TV had been smashed and was on the floor. The front door was ajar! My heart started beating out through my chest.

"Stay here!" I yelled.

I ran into the house with a karate chop at the ready. The front hallway was a complete disaster, junk was scattered everywhere. The lounge room was worse again with cushions akimbo. The backdoor was swaying in the breeze. I sprinted upstairs hoping I'd find it all untouched but of course I was delusional.

Lucy screamed from downstairs, "We've been robbed!"

I shouted from upstairs, "Grab the kids and keep them in the lounge room, Judy, you as well!"

"I will not! I'm getting my slingshot," Judy cried.

"Judy, it's not safe… wait, you have a slingshot? I don't want to know, just stay here with the kids while I take a look."

Everyone was hysterical, the children were screaming, Lucy was in tears and for reasons that still escape me, Judy had a slingshot. We had definitely been done, or as our street would say, 'we'd been Bobbed'. Poor Bob down the road, now I knew how he felt. Everything was in rack and ruin. Even the bottom side of our mattress had been upturned and slashed. The bastards ruined a perfectly good mattress looking for cash, like I stitch it into all my bedding, Escobar style. Idiots!

They started out back kicking through Steve's makeshift wall. Who would've thought replacing a brick wall with chipboard wouldn't be secure? "Just until the bifold doors are ready," he said. 'Yeah or until some prick knocks it down with a sledge hammer looking for loot ya dickhead,' is what hindsight me wishes he could say. My guess is they were after all of Steve's builder gear but there was none to be found as even he didn't trust our neighbourhood and had taken it all away for the weekend. It must've pissed the burglars off. Our makeshift kitchen was decimated, plates broken, a tomato sauce cock and balls was drawn on the wall, despite their anger they really had some artistic flair. The bedroom was worse. All the third draw down gear that was meant for my eyes only, the contents of which included six classic erotic novels I had set aside in case the internet went down, a month's supply of condoms (three condoms – shagger), the vibrator that Lucy didn't want anything to do with, and an unused cock ring I won on a stag do, all hidden safely under a jumper in the third draw down, was now strewn across the floor boards and down the hall for everyone to see. It begged the question, how long had the Bedford Burglar spent in our room? What had they done? We were out all day. They could have got up to all sorts. I felt violated. I still do!

I wish the day got better but despite my best efforts it only got worse.

"What are we going to do?" Lucy was at our bedroom door wiping the tears from her eyes with her hand, because we didn't trust any of the paper in our house, be it tissue or toilet, everything was now suss. I gave her a hug as that's all I could offer and I needed one just as much. The kids joined us wrapping their arms around our legs. Judy, with slingshot in hand, put her arms around the children, and we all stood there and sobbed at what had happened. The grief was real. But someone had to stand up and be strong and lead us out of the crisis and that someone was me.

I thought it best I lay on a speech.

"Guys, no matter what has happened, we still have each other. We have a roof over our heads and love in our hearts. We could say, that whoever did this is a despicable human being but then we'd quickly be overcome by hate. The other option is to think that maybe whoever did this doesn't have it as good as we do, maybe they were desperate. That's how I choose to look at it. I'm going to feel sorry for the burglar because I'd put money on them not having a loving family and a loving home, not having food on their table, not having a life as rich as ours."

Judy chimed in from the stands, "What rubbish! They're thieves and crooks and should be in jail!"

"C'mon, Judy, we can't let them win!"

The kids understood what I meant; I could feel their strength grow with every word.

"We are going to pick ourselves up and carry on. In fact, maybe here and now, we can make a pact to start doing more for our local community because if we help those less fortunate than us, then maybe people won't end up so desperate and feel the need to break into other people's houses."

This was a complete stream of consciousness, a speech for the ages. My ears couldn't believe what my mouth was saying.

"Honey, someone broke into our house and the kids are scared, they don't need Bob Geldof to fix the situation they need to know that they're safe." Lucy always was the sane one.

"Safe? Between my fists of fury and GG's slingshot of death the bad guys don't stand a chance."

"How about I take you children out for dinner while Mummy and Daddy have a clean-up?" Finally, Judy was talking sense.

"Spaghetti Johns?" the kids screamed. Spaghetti Johns was their favourite restaurant because, as the name suggests, they were guaranteed spaghetti.

"Where else? Of course, Spaghetti Johns!" Judy said, she really was great with them.

"Thanks, Mum. Did they take anything of yours?" Lucy asked.

"There's dents in the door so they tried but I put in three padlocks so they didn't stand much of a chance."

"Three padlocks! Jesus, Judy! What have you got up there that would need three padlocks? Every day you're getting a new delivery?" I asked, genuinely wanting to know.

"A clean toothbrush that's what." And with that, Judy smiled and helped the kids back into their shoes and headed out the door.

Lucy and I spent the next two hours putting our gear back on the shelves, fixing cupboards, washing the sheets, figuring out what could and couldn't be saved and also replacing all toothbrushes just in case Judy was right. The hardest part was sifting through the memories. There were the broken seashell's the kids collected on our holiday to Whitstable. Albie's first ever big boy cricket bat that somehow made its way into the shower, the sleep-sock that Marty the Tomato slept in, the candelabra Lucy's dad gave her before we left Australia, the family photo albums! Every item was a reminder of what we had to be grateful for but now it was tarnished and came with a sigh. I'm glad the kids weren't there.

Eventually police arrived. Officer Brady did most of the talking while some lanky bloke powdered for prints. Officer Brady was a dour looking lady who could've easily had a career as a head mistress at an orphanage.

"Any leads?" I asked, having always wanted to do so.

"No, we haven't got any leads. Break-ins can take a long time to solve. Although we have had a few of them in the area so if they're related any clue could lead to a breakthrough."

"Let's hope we catch the Bedford Burglar?" I said, but officer Brady had no idea what I was talking about.

"Right, Mr and Mrs Vincent, according to your

initial statement you came home around five in the afternoon to find the front door ajar and your belongings scattered. Correct?"

"Yes, that's right," said Lucy who was now fresh out of tears.

"And no one else was in the house?"

"Yep that's right, I went and scanned the house, room to room, but they were all clear. My observations have it that they kicked in the back door and went for it," I said in a deep voice.

"Right… it was 'all clear' then… and they 'went for it'," said officer Brady while jotting down my statement with her eyebrows raised, which didn't go unnoticed.

"OK, what we need now is a list of any items that were taken. The list will then be placed into our database and, while we can't promise anything, if the items are ever found or seized it will help us direct them back to you. So, if you could let me know what was taken."

I got the ball rolling, "Right, yes well, the kid's bikes are gone."

Lucy stopped me, "No, we took the bikes to the park remember? They're in the boot."

"Sorry, yes, we have the bikes."

The officer tried to help us along, "What about your computer?"

"The desktop? No that's nearly twelve years old, they didn't touch that."

"Any phones or laptops?"

"No, my laptop's older than my desktop and our phones were in the glove box as it was No Screen Day," I said scratching my head.

"Did they take your TV?"

"No, we've got an old Samsung, it'd cost you more in petrol money to take it to the tip. We're looking at getting new one this Christmas. One of those 4K numbers. Don't tell the kids," I said trying to convince her that we at least had plans on being modern.

"They did knock it over though, cracked the screen," Lucy said, highlighting the damage done.

"That's not great, is it? What about jewellery?"

"No, they left my necklaces on the floor?" Lucy gave the officer a furtive glance, the classic, 'he's a cheap bastard but he means well' look.

I tried to save a bit of face, "They didn't take your necklace? That was a genuine Swarovski. They didn't want it? Odd."

"It was a lookalike, Adam," said Lucy, as Officer Brady offered her a tissue and looked at me with disapproving eyes.

"What about any cash? Did you have money hidden for a rainy day?"

"No, we're not really that kind of family," Lucy said. Now she was almost giggling.

"What about food? Did they take any food?"

"No, I was due to go shopping tomorrow?" I said.

"Nothing from the freezer?"

"Nothing from the freezer."

"So, was anything stolen?" Officer Brady was growing impatient.

"I'm sure something was taken!" I said, looking to Lucy for reassurance.

"I don't know if anything was, Adam. I assumed something of yours was stolen?"

"Is there any reason someone may have wanted to look through your belongings?"

"We're from Australia, we only know a handful of people and they're all decent. Who would do that? Besides we have nothing important, clearly!"

"Yes, it is highly unlikely, they were probably after your workers gear and got carried away but we can't rule anything out. It could be that whoever broke in, was disturbed and fled before taking anything."

"If we tell you they took our new kitchen do you think the house insurance will help us pay for a new one?" I joked, as you do in these dark situations. Went for nothing. Officer Brady just stared at me in, what I'm pretty sure was, disgust.

"That would be illegal. I guess one positive is your new kitchen wasn't ruined."

"Imagine if they destroyed the new warming drawer?" Lucy said.

"You're getting a warming drawer? Very nice. Built in?"

"Built in," Lucy said with pride.

Officer Brady let out a surprised whistle saying, "You lucky devil!"

"I know."

"Lucky? Ladies, can we get back to the destruction of the house? I'm all for a well-timed roast but there is a high probability that someone popped our toothbrushes up their arse!"

"Calm down, Mr Vincent, we're just trying to put a positive spin on things. Now, I doubt anyone would resort to doing such horrible things to your toothbrushes but if you are worried about it, I'd suggest buying new ones. Otherwise, I think my work here is done. Hopefully Ken got some prints but like I said, the good news is nothing thus far seems to have been taken. If you do notice that anything is missing, you can always contact me and I'll add it to the list. Good luck with the warming drawer, Mrs Vincent." The officer looked at Lucy with pity and then went back to her patrol car.

And there it was, total humiliation. Some useless junkie prick risked their life to break into our house only to look around at all of our worldly possessions and say, 'No… there is nothing here good enough for me and my useless junkie prick of a lifestyle'. And then a few hours later our lack of riches was written up in an official police report for everyone to see. Total. Humiliation.

Judy came home not long after the police left and I had to endure another conversation about how nothing I had provided this family was good enough for the depraved. Judy will feed out on this for weeks.

It was such a nice day.

I had lunch in the car with Lizzie while Lucy and Judy reconstructed the makeshift kitchen. Steve fixed us up a new back door, this time with a sturdier lock. The kids aren't happy with his work, they won't go to bed unless we leave saucepans full of water on the ground. 'We'll hear the burglar come in 'is their thinking. Clever. One upshot is Steve reckons the new kitchen will be in next week and the bifold doors a week after that. It was much needed positive news especially after Kevin and Sylvia came around to offer their condolences.

"The burglar didn't take anything?"

"Nothing!"

"Because they took our laptops…"

We know, Sylvia, no need to keep banging on about it!

I'm also now very suss on Judy. It struck me that I don't really know who this woman is. She may be Lucy's mother but she may also be a deranged psycho. It's strange that I just let her move in. No interview process, no due diligence, no phoning for a reference, I just let her waltz right on in and start living up the stairs. I have no idea who I am half the time, so who the hell is Judy? She's nearly in her seventies and lifting weights, she openly carries a slingshot, I've never seen her without makeup and her hair is always set in the same way, a jet black bouffant that must require a load of hair spray, she was rich but now she's broke and yet, somehow the woman needs three padlocks on her door.

Surely she's a genuine fire risk? Which is what I'll say if she catches me breaking into her room tomorrow.

In other news, I've decided to go to a private clinic about my face cancer. They say, 'if you don't have your health you don't have anything' and this robbery has proven that I don't have anything so I may as well have my health.

I deserve more than a 'probably be all right'. Appointment in two days' time. Class.

There's no secrets on this street. Word must have got around that we don't own anything worth stealing so now people are dropping their unwanted goods in our front garden. This morning I found an old laptop and a pair of roller blades on the doorstep with a note, 'For the kids'. Two weeks ago, I was working as a writer at BBC studios and now my neighbours think I'm destitute. Even the Syrian's look at me with pity. As they should, the repair guy charged me two hundred quid to replace the glass on those windows.

I went to the face clinic. I felt guilty that I was somehow betraying the NHS by doing it but then I thought of

Uncle Noel's nose and walked right in.

I was first met by the receptionist, the young and vivacious Jessica. Great with a chat, good with a laugh, was probably at university studying to be more than a receptionist but she cracked on and did her job with a smile because that's what you do when you're in the private sector and you know someone can fire you. Her desk was white and clean like the office that it sat in. There was a living indoor plant and a fish tank that held a number of tropical fish. Classical music played softly over the speakers and the magazines were all up to date. Each chair came with its own USB connector so you could recharge your phone as you waited. Bliss. Not that waiting was a problem. Jessica offered me a green tea and said Doctor Gordon would only be a few more minutes. And she was right. Out he came, all six foot six of his tanned muscle-bound self.

"Hi, I'm Doctor Gordon."

"Hi." That's all I could say, he was too good looking and his teeth were so white I wasn't sure if he was smiling or giving me an X-ray.

His office was much the same as the reception area, only he had a juicer in the corner and wheatgrass growing on the window sill. It was slightly over the top but it gave me confidence and that's what I was paying for. Things only got better when Dr Gordon sat me down and asked me to tell him everything.

He listened to my every word.

"You're right to be worried, Adam. It could be a

nasty spot. I'm going to get a series of blood tests done and then I'm going to send you to my skin guy. Jessica will book you in and give you all the appropriate forms. The most important thing you can do now, is not to worry. OK? We've got this!"

"Thanks, Doctor Gordon."

"Please, call me Jeff."

My new best mate Jeff shook my hand and walked me to Jessica.

"Jess, Adam needs to see Dr Lu, and can we push it through quickly? It was lovely to meet you, Adam, and I'd just like to say, welcome home."

I almost cried. This was the service I was looking for. I'd made a proper man decision and it was medically the right thing to do. Jessica smiled while confirming my details. I smiled back. Finally, actual service.

"We'll email with times and costs later today and hopefully see you before the week is out."

"Thank you, Jessica."

I left feeling great. I'd done something for myself and it was important for my health so I didn't need to feel bad about spending the money. Why would I? I've said from word go, I'm the one who needs to be on the pitch. Do I not deserve private health care? Why should I be the schmuck who waits in line only to be told that things will 'probably be all right?' I'm a go-getter! I go out and get things and bring them back and say, 'look what I've got?' I work in TV, damn it!

Sure enough, that email did come through. The consultation cost me one hundred pounds which I expected but the quote for the biopsy was for nine hundred and fifty quid. Jesus!

My fingers hovered above the keyboard as I contemplated how to respond. It didn't take long for me to type, 'You know what, it will probably be all right.' Then I hit send, mentally waving goodbye to Jessica and Dr Gordon forever, knowing full well that my life was worth less than a grand.

The new cooker is in! We're yet to have the cupboards, drawers, sink or worktop installed but Houston, we have a cooker! Had we waited three more days Steve would've finished the job but Lucy had it in her head that today was the day she was using the new stove.

I don't blame her. We've had months of cooking on a portable one hob burner. When I picked it up for thirty quid on Facebook Marketplace the bloke I bought it from couldn't look me in the eye. After a month of eating half cooked pasta and lukewarm stew I now know why. Last night's dish was the final straw for all of us. Judy served us up gruel. You put a spoonful in your mouth and your natural reaction was to speak in tongues as if possessed. A fair reaction given it was the culinary equivalent of Satan exploding his arse into your bowl.

Judy claimed she cooked it from scratch but earlier, when trying to create more room in the recycling bin, I found two empty tins of Irish stew. The cheeky liar! I'll be keeping that up my sleeve for when she next attacks my character. Even me, with my working-class background, scoffs at tinned Irish stew. Judy really lowered her colours and today was Lucy's chance to put her family name back in the good cookbooks. She went for it.

The bathroom was cordoned off and a runway from sink to stove was cleared. No one was allowed to enter. It was too dangerous. The famous warming drawer that had been the topic of every second discussion in my life for the previous six months, was now placed precariously on a workmen's makeshift bench top. Delivered with the stove, Lucy had Steve wire both items up so now she was not only oven ready, she was warming drawer ready.

Lucy took no prisoners, running back and forth from bathroom to kitchen emptying pans, straining greens, opening windows to clear steam, stirring and whirring, bashing and crashing, all five hob rings were on the go. The oven pre-heated almost instantly, and unlike the last one it no longer needed a chair to prop the door shut. Lucy even managed to use that side oven, to crisp the potatoes and carrots. So, I guess that's what it's for, crisping? Glad we spent the money. After hours of hustle and bustle Lucy served up the most delicious succulent roast chicken with golden brown potatoes (thanks side stove), caramelised carrots and parsnips and corn on the cob and freshly steamed greens and, my God, it was a magnificent spread. The previous month of eating slop was officially over, Judy's horrendous dish was one bowel movement away from being long forgotten and this roast was a chance to taste our future and the future tasted great. Within a week we'll be eating on a table in our new open plan kitchen diner, no longer in the front lounge-room displayed like zoo animals for all passers-by to gawk at. All five of us sat around the table and devoured our first properly hot meal in months. No one spoke, we were too busy chewing. Our curtains were open but nobody cared, let the onlookers look. It was feeding time and the food was only getting better.

Once we cleared the table and washed the pots, pans and plates in the bathroom sink, a system we had grown accustomed to throughout the months, with me washing, Judy wiping, the kids running dishes to Lucy who would place them back on the makeshift kitchen cupboard, which was actually the lounge room sideboard. Once that process was over, we fell into hysterics playing the game, 'What's in the warming drawer?' Lucy had kept it as a surprise all day, so the anticipation of what was in the warming drawer had us all wondering.

"What's in the warming drawer?" I'd ask, the kids having no idea I was pretending to be Brad Pitt from the movie Seven.

"Ice cream!" Lizzie shouted.

"In a warming drawer? It would melt, duh," said Albie.

"OK, Mr Smarty Pants, your turn, what's in the warming drawer?"

"Um, it's a teleporting machine where all parents get sucked in and then, skip ad, let me spend the rest of my life playing Fortnite and, skip ad, where I get a million subs, I like your cut, G," responded Albie, and I still have no idea what he actually meant.

"A monkey!" said Lizzie.

"Lucy, is it a monkey?" I called.

"No, it's not a monkey," Lucy yelled back.

"OK then, Judy, your turn, what's in the warming drawer?"

"I don't know but it smells lovely?"

"So do babies. Kids, is a baby in the warming drawer?"

"Noooo!" They yelled.

"OK, kids… a drum roll please, here we go, for the final time, Lucy, what's in the warming drawer?"

The kids and I went full drum roll while giggling hysterically, Judy joined in and we all stomped our feet waiting for the big reveal. Poor Lucy had to leave the makeshift lounge room dining area and hightail it the kitchen, open up the drawer, take whatever it was out, then come all the way back, minding not to trip over the workmen's remaining gear. It was quite a drum roll.

"Cheesecake!" yelled Lucy, entering the room half

puffed from the journey. The kids went crazy and ran around the room, jumping on the couch like they'd just scored the winning goal at Wembley. It was a mad house and I loved every second of it. Then a fuse blew and all the lights went off because the rules clearly state that I cannot have a good time. What was in the warming drawer? It turns out it was poor wiring and shoddy workmanship. Not that I mind, the best memories are often the ones that don't go to plan.

Lucy and I finished our mid-morning cup of tea and then had a secret pow wow in the bathroom. This chat was long overdue.

"It's Mum's room, we can't just barge in."

"Sure we can, she doesn't pay rent, legally I think we have grounds to evict her!"

"Very funny."

"I wasn't going for laughs. Don't you want to know why your mum needs three padlocks on her door? One padlock is fine but three? She's told the kids they're not allowed in her room. It's rude. And why has she suddenly decided it's important to be able to twang someone in the head with a ball bearing from three hundred yards? Why is she only just covering her food and bills but offering no help on the mortgage as promised? And this 'why 'puzzles me the most, why does she have a constant stream of parcels, some of which are suspiciously heavy, arriving on an almost daily basis?"

"Not daily?"

"Yes, daily! Often timed perfectly with my afternoon nap. I've shat myself so many times from Derek's loud knocking that it's moved my cycle."

"You're on a first name basis with the delivery guy?"

"Yes! So can we please see what all the boxes are about?"

"What's in the box?" Lucy said doing a much better impersonation of Brad Pitt than I had managed.

"Very clever."

After two hours of subtle manipulation, which involved conversations around 'active people living longer' Judy decided she would take a walk around Bedford Park. Once the coast was clear Lucy agreed that perhaps this was an emergency and decided to use the 'in case I die keys' that Judy had recently bequeathed her. We snuck upstairs and stood at the landing, keys in hand, not at all ready for what we were about to find.

"Holy shit!" Lucy gasped.

This was indeed a holy shit moment. Judy's entire room was filled with bottled water, tins, and you couldn't move for rice. There must have been a hundred small bags of the stuff stacked neatly beside her bed, making the loft look like a makeshift bomb shelter from World War Two. How she got two giant blue plastic drums upstairs without us noticing is beyond me but there they were filled with wholegrain and doubling up as bedside tables. Her dresser was covered in supplements. She had all the vitamins there, A through K, as well as fish oil, hemp oil, flaxseed. I saw a container of creatine and one of those huge tubs of protein powder that only weightlifters and men experiencing a midlife crisis use. My kettle bells were at the end of her bed next to four first-aid kits and an inversion bench. You'd think her hanging upside down all day like a bat would be the weirdest discovery but no, on her table were two computer screens, a handheld radio and an unopened box containing night vision goggles.

"I think your mum's a prepper!"

"I think you're right."

"She's sixty-eight! What can she possibly be preparing for?"

"I don't know."

I pulled a can from the top of her stash. "Here's that Irish stew she served the other night. She's been using us to rotate her tins."

"Why does she have four first-aid kits?"

"What about the goggles? Maybe your mum is James Bond!"

"And the handheld radio? None of this makes sense…"

"Maybe she's been making money talking dirty to truck drivers?"

"Stop it, Adam, this isn't funny, I'm scared!" Lucy was looking very perturbed, like the curtain had been pulled back and the emperor was wearing fully camouflaged underpants and a tin foiled hat.

Lucy and I sat on the end of Judy's bed and waited like concerned parents for her to return. I tried on the goggles and they really do work. Lucy refused to show me her infrared boobies. She was too concerned to be playful, so I hung upside down in the dark with the goggles on. Then Judy walked in and nearly blinded me.

"Ow! Jesus, Judy! Switch the light off. Lucy, can you help me…"

"Mum, you have a lot of explaining to do," said Lucy, while helping me into an upright position.

"You broke into my room! How dare you?"

"It's our room, Judy, we let you sleep in it for free, you have no legal right…"

"Mum, what is all of this?"

"It's none of your business, that's what it is," Judy said somewhat defiantly even though she clearly knew she was in the wrong.

"You fed us Irish stew, Judy, and claimed it as your own, despite it tasting like sh…"

"I had to rotate the tins!"

"Didn't I tell you?" I said looking at Lucy like I'd just told her.

"Rotate the tins! Mum, what are you talking about?"

I wasn't going to beat around the bush, "Are you a

prepper, Judy? Is that what all this is? You think the world is going to end?" I picked up the handheld radio. "Breaker, breaker Judy has lost the plot, over."

"Adam, stop it!" Lucy wasn't happy with my line of attack.

"No, I do not think the world is going to end but yes I do prepare for when the banks might collapse."

"The banks? Mum, what are you on about?"

"Darling, I've seen the videos, I know what's coming. I wasn't ready for when your father left me financially ruined but I'll be damned if I walk into the next collapse unprepared."

"Mum, what are you talking about? What's coming is us looking after you," Lucy pleaded, looking for an ounce of sanity.

"Oh, don't be a fool! Don't you realise how close you are to losing everything? Your husband writes jokes about steak knives in the front seat of his car for Christ's sake! You're up to your eye balls in debt. You know he cries on the toilet?" Judy yelled unnecessarily, pointing directly at me.

"Given our recent poor diet I think we've all shed a few tears on the toilet, Judy, and those jokes have been paying the bills! Plus, I've got my stand up. Don't you worry about me, I've got some irons in the fire."

"But I do worry, Adam, constantly. Can't you see the governments are losing control, they're printing money like it's water and one day soon it will all collapse."

"How much time are you spending online, Judy? You sound like you've been watching David Icke."

"Mock me all you want but it's happening."

"Mum, why didn't you tell us you were worried?" Lucy asked.

"Because I wanted to protect you from the outside world. If anyone found out about the stockpile, then we'd be a security risk. To think the burglars almost got away with the lot."

"Yeah they really missed out on that stew," I said.

"How did you pay for all of this, Mum?" Lucy asked.

"I've been using my pension. I did buy the computers on credit but only because I can't see Miles on my phone, it's my eyes, they struggle with the screen, vitamin A helps... I have no idea how to use the damn thing..." Judy tapped the computer. "... I was meaning to ask you for help, Lucy, but..." And then she broke down in tears on the bed... "... I'm not ready to die." The woman was a mess. "... I miss your dad so much," Lucy held her and they both cried. I watched over them wearing the night vision goggles.

Four cups of strong herbal tea and a fresh box of tissues later and we had almost removed the doom from Judy's noggin. At the heart of the issue is her loneliness and anger. She misses Lucy's dad but is angry at him for leaving her with nothing. At one point she cried out, "We had a great life, we used to have dinner with the Franklins but now it's all gone!" I assume the Franklins

207

were their version of the Luptons, a signpost that pointed to better times. "Lucy, you were supposed to get half the house." That's when the tears hit me. What we could've done with that money. She'd been with us for what felt like an age and I had completely forgotten that her world had been turned upside down. From riches to rags isn't how most of us want to go. Not that living in Bedford was impossible to deal with, but when you used to spend your Australian winters in the south of France it's a definite step down. I felt sorry for her, then she mentioned Miles.

For some crazy reason Judy is completely guilt ridden that she has abandoned her bong smoking loser son. Miles is a fully grown thirty-six-year-old man-child who sells stamps from his girlfriend's basement. He hooked up with a middle-aged Korean lady who loves that he owns Elvis stamps. They met online, she's a mad Elvis fan, and he wowed her with six original Elvis stamps from the seventies. A quick search on eBay shows you they're worth about two hundred quid but it was enough to light Lee Jin's fire and now Miles sniffs his own farts while hocking The King from her couch. I may well be a dickhead but at least I make an effort. This dipshit is useless. He regularly posts on Facebook about how the global financial system is set to collapse and the New World Order will soon be upon us. Any conspiracy nut worth their lizard skin would rather be doxed as a government spy than openly post on Facebook. Miles is an amateur. The real conspiracy is that he's been radicalising his own mum, emailing her clips about financial doom and gloom while contributing three parts of fuck all to her welfare. All while she gives me grief for putting a roof over her head. The poor woman hangs on his every word. I assume it's because she wants to be there when he 'turns his life around' which explains all the supplements. Judy must know she is going to have to live until she's a hundred and ten before Miles sorts himself out. And even then…

Gave the night goggles a spin in the park after dark. They work but you do get some looks.

I did my good deed for the day and gave Omar our shitty electrical hob. I'm sure he'll find a use for it. Luke-warm stew for me is probably a hot roast for him. The poor bloke struggled to find the words but when he finally said, 'thank you' I got a lump in my throat. A toothless refugee, living in borderline squalor in HMO housing, his kids run around in second hand shoes and yet I've made his day with an old hob. Between me paying up on our last bet, which still stings, and today's free cooker, they must think I'm some kind of God. It feels good to be good.

Kids are wondering why we keep having rice for dinner. I haven't got the heart to tell them.

▄▄▄▖▗▄▚▞▀▙▘▗▀▜▞▀▙▞▀▟▚▀▙▄▄

Albie had his first official tournament this afternoon, The County Closed Tennis Championships. Garry Foxe and his squad of up and comers were pitting their skills against the best coaches and players Bedfordshire had to offer and I couldn't wait. Knowing that the penny would soon drop and these idiot parents would finally realise their precious little children don't have what it takes. That they've actually been conned out of thousands of pounds by a conniving coach; knowing that we were only two or three games away from experiencing a disappointed dad conniption, well that had me on the edge of my seat. Lucy was there and we huddled under a blanket. Me, knowing the truth, her, overly optimistic that her boy stood a chance.

"Now you know he may not be any good," I said trying to manage expectations.

"He'll be great. Garry tells me he's really come on."

"I bet he did."

Lucy then lent over and whispered into my ear like a playful child.

"Dear Adam's Brain, I think you should stop being a cynical dickhead and appreciate that you're sitting under a blanket with your wife and that you get to watch your son play a sport he enjoys, love from Lucy's Brain."

She smiled and I couldn't hide my own big cheesy grin. Whispering to each other's brain was a trope from our early dating days. She always knew when to bring it back, and how to drag me away from the precipice of self-importance. That she did it by the side of a tennis court on a cold Bedford morning made it all the better.

"Let's go, Albie!" I yelled.

"Go get 'em, Albie!" Lucy cheered.

The other parents tutted with disapproval clearly not appreciating that we'd just had a moment.

"Seriously though, he might be rubbish."

"Oh shut up, you big stupid rabbit," said Lucy, playfully elbowing me in the shoulder.

Garry stood court side clapping the players on, no doubt nervous because today's results would dictate his income stream for the remainder of the year. If his kids performed, the parents would keep coughing up, it was that simple and boy did he start with a howler. Ten minutes into round one, and one of the dads was loudly protesting a line call from an opposition player.

"That was in! Rodney, stick up your racket and let the coach know."

"It's the players call, we ask that the parents not get involved," said Garry firmly to the dad.

Poor Rodney was down five-love and his old-man was livid. Unfortunately I didn't get to enjoy the fullness of Rodney Senior's anger because Albie, had already come bounding back.

"I won my first match, Dad, two-love."

"Well done, Albie," Lucy said looking at me with an 'I told you so' face.

"That was quick. Two sets to you?"

"Yep, I'm playing again in five minutes. Far court. Keep watching me." And he ran off without a care in the world.

"We will. Enjoy!" said Lucy, not realising the gravity of the situation.

Then Garry popped over to make it worse. "He looks like he's having fun."

"How'd you get on with that other dad?" I asked, hoping he'd show me a black eye.

"Fine. Sometimes the parents can get a bit too involved and you have to have a quiet word and remind them that it's only a game."

"Exactly!" said Lucy.

"Expensive game though, isn't it?"

Lucy elbowed me in the shoulder but this time she meant it.

Unfortunately, for my wallet, Albie went on to win his next match as well. Beginner's luck? Ideally you want them beating a couple of losers, and then to get thumped by the big boys. That way your kid walks away happy that they weren't the worst but also realising they'll never have what it takes. That's the win-win every parent is hoping for. I hadn't planned for Albie to reach the quarter-finals.

"This is a disaster," I said to Lucy.

"Why? He's done really well."

"If he keeps going like this he'll think he's in with a chance."

"But he is in with a chance."

"Yeah, a chance of wanting more lessons."

"So?"

"We can't afford the lessons!"

"Oh, stop being a downer. We'll find a way. Maybe I could coach him? Take a leaf out of Judy Murray's book."

I couldn't give that the response it deserved as Albie ran over beaming, "I'm into the quarter-finals, Dad!"

"That's brilliant, Albie," I lied.

"Here's a snack and don't forget to keep hydrated," Lucy said, summoning the spirit of Judy Murray.

"Thanks, Mum." And again, he was off to play with his mates.

Garry gave me a thumbs up from a distance with his standard raised eyebrow theatrics, like he'd given birth to a new Nadal.

Albie's quarter-final opponent was a boy called Ace. Ace, seriously? Do we need more evidence that tennis parents are psychopaths? This kid's life looked like it had been planned from the womb. He walked onto court with a tennis bag that was twice his size, wearing sun glasses that covered three quarters of his face, and sporting bright fluorescent orange tennis shoes that probably cost more than my car. You don't drop this much money on a kid who can't play. There was no shame in Albie losing to this prodigal son. But Albie didn't get that message because he went out there and bamboozled the spoilt little brat. I couldn't believe it. He absolutely smashed him. Forehands, backhands, volleys, Albie was playing out of his skin. So much so that Ace started throwing his racket, crumbling under the pressure of his own name. Really his parents should've called him Double Fault because he whacked down five in a row and gave my boy the match.

Lucy couldn't believe it, "He's into the semi-final! He's into the semi-final! Adam, he's into…"

"The semi-final, yes I know. It was a great win, wasn't it? Well-done, Albie!" I shouted across the court through gritted teeth while sneering at Ace as he slunk past. That win alone would see Albie playing for another six months. Ace had just cost us hundreds.

Lucy was beside herself with joy. "No one in our family has made a semi-final of anything. When Garry said he was good I didn't think he was this good."

"I must admit, today is the best I've seen him."

"Dear Adam's Brain, I told you so."

The drama and tension of Bedfordshire's under ten County Closed Tennis Tournament reached fever pitch when Albie discovered his semi-final opponent would be none other than, The Red Headed Ringer. I couldn't believe my luck, finally after all this time the other

214

parents would have their own Keyser Soze moment and realise that the nuff their kids regularly beat in practice was actually a mini Federer. And The Ringer was underplaying his hand beautifully. No big bag, no designer sunglasses, no flashy shoes; the kid was here to win and poor Albie had no idea.

"Dad, if I win this I'm into the final."

"You just have fun, mate, I'm proud of you no matter what."

"We both are, sweetheart, now don't be afraid to put a bit of top spin into your forehand and don't get stuck on that baseline," said Lucy, who had spent the last ten minutes You Tubing tennis tactics.

"I won't, Mum. Wish me luck."

"Good luck!"

And with that our boy was off.

The crowd gathered. Some were interested in who would make the final, others were keen to find out just what it was their kid didn't have. Garry stood court-side looking sheepish, his crimes were about to be revealed. There was no hiding that The Ringer could play and his long con was about to come undone on the main court. This was suburban tennis at its finest.

Albie won the toss, serving first. An ace down the T sets the tone and he holds his first game comfortably. Swapping ends it's The Ringer's turn. He serves his own ace, and follows the next point up with a sliced serve that Albie hits into the net. Too much top spin on that one. Realising The Ringer is way better than they thought, the parents of Bedford's tennis community begin to talk. But their murmurs turn into outright applause as the red head finesses a stunning backhand down the line. How did he get to that? Garry hides in plain sight by clapping the shot. Disgusting. But the crowd is too enthralled with these under tens to concern themselves with the justified paranoia emanating from my crazy dad mind. They whoop and cheer every shot the two boys play, and why wouldn't they? The shots are glorious. Be it an exquisite drop from Albie or The Ringer's cross court forehand, there really is no looking away. But Albie blinks first, volleying into the net and giving up the first set.

The boys take a well-earned drink as a toddler runs onto the court carrying a sandwich. Tomato falls onto the playing surface but is quickly mopped up with a wet wipe from an apologetic mum. This match has everything. Back for the opening of set two.

The Ringer serves an almighty ace and holds his game comfortably. They again swap ends and a nervous Albie looks to his dad for confidence. His dad gives him the knowing nod that he learnt how to do from Omar during Football-Gate. With Dad on side, Albie launches a barrage of his own aces and it's clear we have ourselves a match. The crowd is heaving now and they can't pick a winner, nor do they want one. Both players deserve to taste victory. If this is the semi what will the final have to offer? The Ringer faces his first challenge and goes down a break point. If he can't hold here then surely the momentum is all with Albie. The Ringer serves, Albie hits a stunner down the line, but the red headed nut bar and his jungle cat reflexes see the ball back over the net and he goes on to hold the game. Now Albie must serve to stay in the match. He starts well, taking it to thirty love, then double faults before hitting a back hand into the net. The Ringer is close to victory here, hitting his now trade mark cross court forehand, the one Garry has been paying him to withhold from the local gullible parents. He hits that money maker into the top left of the court and has himself a match point. Unbelievable scenes! Albie has played one hell of a match and really made his parents proud, especially his dad who gave him no chance. But even he must sense that the end is near. Albie serves it wide and rushes to the net hoping for an easy volley but the Ringer mishits it and it goes over Albie's head only to land safely in the court. And that's the match! It's an anticlimactic end to an otherwise skilful display from two kids who, let's face it, will never be good enough or rich enough to ever have a serious crack at this posh boys sport called tennis.

Lucy was in tears. "You did so well, Albie."

Albie was in tears. "I played terribly."

"Terribly? You were brilliant!" I said, wiping dust from my eye.

"No, I served a double fault. I was rubbish!" Albie

said, now properly crying in his mother's arms.

Noticing the tears, Garry chimed in with some support, "Albie, that was brilliant. That boy Henry, he's one of the best in the country and you almost won. Wow! What a match! High five!"

Albie's spirits lifted.

"Can I go to the canteen and get a juice?"

"Of course you can," Lucy said handing him some money. Albie ran off which Garry saw as an opportunity to give us 'the speech'.

"Guys, this was the perfect tournament. You don't want him winning because he'd get bored, coming third leaves him hungry. Plus Henry is in the top fifty in the country for his age and Albie didn't lose by much. Didn't I tell you he had talent? And that is him only having one lesson a week. Imagine what he's going to do when he starts doing two lessons a week? We'll definitely have him join the county squad in Luton on Sunday mornings."

"Sunday mornings? Luton?" I yelled.

"That's the only place we can find indoor courts."

"We'll be there," Lucy said, clearly falling for his sales pitch.

"We will?" I said, not believing a word of it. "Hey Garry, I've seen Albie beat that red headed kid at practice. Only, when I saw him at practice he was hopeless. But today he was brilliant. Why is that? Hmmm?" I said loud enough to try and lure any other disgruntled parents into an argument that nobody else wanted to have.

"You get that with kids, some days they're just off the boil. Consistency comes with age."

"Well, they both played well, didn't they?" said Lucy, hoping her chipper smile would diffuse the situation.

"It really would be good to see him at Luton on Sundays," said Garry, the coach with the vulpine smile. "The sessions are somewhat subsidised."

"Somewhat subsidised! It costs us to play county tennis?" I gasped.

"Well, sign us up, Garry. Albie will love it!" Lucy's chipper smile was now working overtime.

"He really will. And that he came within a whisker of beating one of the best under ten's in the country should give him loads of confidence. I'll leave you to it but really consider giving him some more lessons." And with that, Garry Foxe walked into the dispersing crowd knowing his income was safe for another year. I was gutted. Even the loser dad, Rodney Senior, sucked up to him asking if there was any room in his Bedford squad. Madness.

"Albie was very good," Lucy said, snuggling up to me.

"Rafael Nadal was beating teenagers when he was ten. I don't want to give the kid false hope. Plus the money…"

"We'll find the money, you'll just have to write more worm farm jokes."

"Can't wait."

We headed home with Albie buzzing, Lucy beaming but I was suspicious. If you're one of the top players in the country, why don't you have a tennis bag? Every other kid was carrying a sport bag and a designer drink bottle. They all wore the latest in designer sneakers. All except for Albie and The Ringer. Albie made sense because why would I waste the money but if The Ringer had previously proven himself surely he'd at least have a tennis bag? So when I got home I looked up his ranking. Henry isn't in the top fifty under ten players in the country. He comes in at number seventy-eight.

That Garry Foxe is an absolute shyster.

The day started well, but then Judy had me flipping my lid.

Glen must have called over night from Thailand because I've woken up with his message, "No fuck'n guarantees, cunt, but looks like we scored a fuck'n contract with a chain of bloody fuck'n furniture warehouses. Yet to sign but it'd be six solid fuck'n weeks of running around like a goose filming in Britain's backwater shitholes, might even do Bedford, so think me up some ideas will you, cunt?"

As per, Glen's voice cut through me like a happy

chainsaw. It was good news as long as I didn't mind him dismembering my soul. I didn't of course because I had bills to pay, so I headed out to my last ever day in the car office. That was another piece of positive news. Builder Steve and his crew have spent the last few days putting the finishing touches on our overly priced kitchen and as of tomorrow, I get my old office back. With more work on the go, my old office to look forward to and Lucy finally getting to see our new kitchen, things were looking up. And Graham's back from his trip overseas so we're catching up tomorrow. For a few hours life was good, I was in the zone but then I looked up and in my rear vision mirror I saw Judy walking towards the house carrying our old portable hob. I opened the car door and confronted her on the street.

"Judy, why are you carrying our old hob?"

"I'm doing no such thing. This a totally different hob?"

"No, Judy, it's the exact the same hob, I just got rid of the damn thing!"

"It's not the same hob. I got this on Facebook Marketplace… for my upstairs kitchenette."

"Your upstairs kitchenette?"

"Yes, my upstairs kitchenette! I want to live independently, give you and the kids some space."

"We don't need… why didn't you just ask to have the hob?"

"Because you have your hob and I want my hob!"

"It's the same bloody hob, Judy!"

"No, it isn't. I bought this one from Omar... the stupid idiot hasn't worked out our currency yet and thinks it's only worth thirty pounds. Thirty pounds... what a bargain!"

"Jesus, Judy, I only just gave it to Omar, for free."

Suddenly I had Lucy at my elbow. "What is all the yelling about?"

"Your mum just bought back our old hob."

"It's not the same hob!"

"That is our hob. I know that hob. I cooked on it for the last six weeks and that is definitely our hob," said Lucy with utter disdain.

"Told you, it's the same one I gave to Omar."

"Why did you give it to Omar?" Lucy asked.

"Because he looks destitute which makes me feel guilty, so I thought maybe it'd help if he had it."

"But it's a terrible hob. And if Mum wanted it, why didn't you just give it to her?" Lucy didn't really see my point.

"I didn't know she wanted a shitty old hob, that's why!"

Omar was now at the end of the street looking at us squabbling, no doubt chuckling at our misfortune.

"Nice one, mate!..." I yelled. "... Love your work, taking advantage of an old lady like that, very clever." And then I clapped him. I once received a long-distance clap and it really got under my skin and I was hoping my clap would do the same.

"So, this is your old hob?" Judy asked.

"Yes!" Lucy and I said in unison.

"That bastard sold me your old hob?" Judy scowled in Omar's direction. He pretended to look elsewhere.

"Yes! But it was your old hob too, Judy. It was yours, mine, ours, the kids. We're a team and as captain of that team, can you please put that bloody hob down!"

"Yes, Mum, put it down. I'm captain, by the way," Lucy said.

"So, I should cancel the solar panels I found on eBay?"

"Mum!"

"Well, if the power goes down, how will we cook our food?"

"Jesus, Judy!"

It may take us a while to get Judy back into the real world. We left the hob on the side of the road. I'm sure Omar grabbed it and got his kid to put it straight back on Facebook. Total hob knob!

We had our last dinner in the lounge room. Lizzie asked us if she could have tennis lessons because she wants to be like Albie. "We can't afford to have two tennis players in the same house, one of you is going to have to get a job." A classic dad line, slightly cynical, more amusing than funny, at best it gets a groan but sometimes that's all you need. I thought nothing of it, until Judy said, "Well I could always sell some of my Bitcoin?"

I mean, who is this woman?

Judy goes on to tell us that Miles gifted her five Bitcoins a while back. The woman who re-purchased our old hob has had tens of thousands of pounds sitting on what looks like a USB stick this entire time. This burns twice, because not only could she have sent a few of those dollars our way, but her loser son could well be minted with Bitcoin too. Yet here I am doing all the heavy lifting. What an arsehole!

***

Graham knocked on our door wearing his blue tracksuit and holding another pie.

"Chicken and veggie and I've got to be honest, I nearly didn't give it to you because it smells too good!"

"Thanks, Graham...," Lucy said taking the pie. "... You boys off for a walk?"

"Yes, can Adam come out to play?" Graham asked with a cheeky smile.

Lucy joined in, "Do you want go and play with Graham, Adam?"

"I'll be back late," I said putting on my headband. "Don't worry, I'll have him back for dinner," Graham said, putting on his.

It was nice just to talk shit with someone again. That's what I miss most about my pre-dad life, the ability to just head out with a mate and talk shit.

"You were robbed and they didn't take anything?"

"Nothing!"

Graham stopped mid-stride and doubled over with laughter. "You poor bastard!"

"Literally, I'm a poor bastard!"

"And Judy is a prepper?"

"Mate, I'll be eating rice for the next twenty years!"

Graham remained in hysterics.

It felt like a good time to bring up the status of his marriage. "How was the Grand Canyon?"

"It does exactly what it says on the tin, it was grand. Jess and I had the best time. She was right all along, it's exactly what we needed. Who would've thought staring into a giant hole would fix a marriage? But it did. It's amazing. We're totally insignificant, Adam. The earth just doesn't care and once you realise that, your problems fade away."

"I should give it a go."

"I don't think it would work for you… you'd need a much bigger hole," Graham laughed.

"Cheeky bugger."

We carried on walking and talking along the east-bank of the river, over the High Street bridge, and back up passed the hubbub of the rowing teams by the boat shed towards the Butterfly Bridge. Our strides weren't as long as they had been on previous walks, which I put down to Graham having just spent three days on a horse, but my gosh we laughed. Graham impersonating his American tour guide has set me right for another six months.

"The Canyon was forged from over hundreds of thousands of years of erosion. Water would come down and... Stop, mate! You're describing a hole! Have some self-respect. The entire point of the Canyon is to show us how brief our lives are and to maybe not waste it on a career describing the transient nature of dirt. Honestly, Adam, had I thought I had any chance of getting back on, I would've hopped off my horse and given the miserable sod a hug. He made you look successful."

Our laughter was abruptly broken when we heard yelling from the Butterfly Bridge. Groups of people were forming at either end, all concerned at what looked like a man standing on the middle of the bridge's outer wires.

"This doesn't look good," said Graham and we both headed over.

The man was standing on the outside of the railing with a heavy chain and what looked like a weighted disk, the sort you'd see at the gym, wrapped around his waist. People kept their distance, but everyone was looking in his direction. Some had their hands on their heads worried sick with fear, others were calling the police, with the odd idiot trying to film it. I was immediately struck by how familiar the guy looked.

"I know this guy, Graham. I've met him

somewhere."

"Then we should get closer. Maybe you can help?"

"The police are on their way," said an onlooker, as Graham and I inched our way through the mob. We managed to get ourselves within metres of where the man stood.

"Don't come near me," he shouted.

"Craig? Craig, is that you? I knew you looked familiar. We met at the Lupton party. We were best mates for two hours, you climbed the giraffe."

Craig slowly turned his head away from the water beneath, our eyes met and he gave me half a nod before re-focussing on the water.

He was frenetic, almost speaking in tongues, "She's gone... She left... I'm so tired... I can't sleep... the kids."

"Who's gone, Craig?"

"Everyone."

"I'm here," I said trying to be positive.

"So am I," said Graham.

"It is Craig, isn't it?" I asked, trying to get him to engage.

"I climbed up the giraffe and you ran down Tavistock Street naked."

"Tavistock Street naked? I don't recall that one." I had no idea what he was talking about but I'm glad he was talking.

"I climbed the giraffe but I've seen CCTV footage of you running naked down Tavistock Street. You were on some kind of Dad's Night and now it's on YouTube. It's definitely you."

"Oh, this sounds amazing. Craig, you don't know me, and I'm sorry to get involved in your suicide attempt, but I have to know where to find this YouTube clip."

"Graham! Now isn't the time!" I yelled.

"There's never a good time to run naked down Tavistock Street, Adam, which is why I must see this clip," Graham said nervously smiling but also slowly working his way closer to Craig.

"Stay there! I'll do it," yelled Craig. He lurched forwards from the wires, the weight around his waist now just inches from the water.

"This clip on YouTube, how many people have seen it?" I asked, partly because I was interested but mainly because I wanted him to keep talking.

"Hundreds."

"And what happened?"

"You jumped naked out of a bin and then ran down the road holding your clothes above your head."

"And you don't remember any of this? Adam, I didn't have you for a blackout drunk," said Graham still moving closer.

"I vaguely remember going for a jog."

"Guys, I know what you're doing. Now stop!"

"You don't want to do this, Craig. No matter how bad your life is now, trust me when I say, it can get better, I promise," I said.

"Jane wants me out, they'd all be better off, I'm so tired. I yell all the time! I'm no good to anyone."

"I'm sure she doesn't want you out, Craig, and we all get mad. Every morning I hear this guy yelling at his kids from across the street," said Graham, his hands now moving along the wires.

"You can hear me getting cranky?"

"You yelling at Albie to hurry up and get dressed is my alarm clock. So don't worry about your yelling, Craig, it can't be worse than his."

"But I don't get to see my kids," Craig stammered.

"Not if you jump, Craig. You won't if you jump. Besides, Adam's kids can't stand him. Really, they make him work from his car," joked Graham easing his way through the wires to stand only a metre to Craig's right.

"Not a step closer or I'm in."

"It's true, Craig, I have to work from my car."

"You know his life is so terrible that a burglar broke into his house and didn't steal anything because they couldn't find anything of value."

"Ease up, Graham, or you'll have me jumping in. Listen, Craig, you have a boy and girl, don't you? I remember from the party, they're beautiful kids and normally I can't stand other people's kids." I was trying to take Craig's gaze from the water.

"I can't," cried Craig, his breathing was deeper now but still erratic.

Taking a leaf out of Graham's book, I crept through

the wires and got within leaping distance of Craig. I was petrified. Not only because I didn't fancy my chances in the river, but also because of my history of saying exactly the wrong thing at the wrong time when people were struggling.

"You just need a good night's sleep, mate. It's all fixable, all of it. And that's coming from a guy who will soon have to explain to his wife that he's on the internet naked."

"I need to end the cycle that's what I need. Every time I try and change I end up right back here!" Craig yelled, but he was posturing to jump. He was heaving his torso back and forward, his arms stretched behind him, each thrust testing his grip of the wire, the dangling weight now splashing in and out of the water. If it snagged on a drifting log he was in. My words were only making it worse. I stepped back and tried to take the pressure off.

I'm convinced what happened next was a divine intervention, a miracle of light that I hope to never forget. The setting sun planted its golden rays on Graham's face transforming his look to that of an enlightened luminous old sage. Sure, a sage that was dressed in a blue tracksuit with mismatching head band but a sage nonetheless. What was even more incredible was how Graham's voice softened with the light, becoming calmer and deeper, as if he were Moses on the hill.

"Craig, I need you to look me in the eye. I know

what you're going through. The headaches from the not sleeping, that heaviness that comes from being over tired and feeling useless, seeing no way out. And the more you try to sleep the harder it gets and if you tell someone it just sounds like you're complaining. You spend your entire day just seeping energy, your mind glitches uncontrollably, and it's terrifying which is why you lash out at those you love. Not because you're angry but because you're scared and desperate for it all to end, for the madness to stop. And when no one understands and the pain outweighs your options that's when you end up here. But I understand, Craig. I had all the same feelings. I may not have been as committed to the cause as you but the same dark thoughts went through my mind and I was terrified. You're not alone, Craig."

With these words Graham, still holding on to the outer wires of the Butterfly Bridge, gently put his left hand on Craig's shoulder.

"I'm not going to stop you from jumping in, but I am going to ask that you please don't. Please. Your kids love you and they need their dad. They do. They love you, Craig. I have no doubt that your wife loves you. I love you. Everyone on this bridge loves you. And we all desperately want you to come back. Will you do that, Craig? Will you step through these wires with me?"

With the evening light guiding his path, Craig carefully undid his weight belt and let it drop into the river before gently easing his body through the wires back onto the safety of the bridge where he fell into

Graham's arms and wept.

"It's OK, son, it's OK. It's only going to get better from now on."

Sirens crept closer from the distance but the only noise that mattered was the muffled wailing of Craig into Graham's shoulder. The rest of us stood in silence as his tears echoed across the water.

The police eventually arrived, and then the ambulance and then it was over, the crowd dispersed having seen enough action for one day. Graham joined Craig in the back of the ambulance and they headed off to the hospital. I met them there to see that he got properly checked out but after two hours of waiting in A&E Craig decided it might be best if he self-discharge and we go to the pub for a quiet chat.

"You really saw CCTV footage of me running naked down Tavistock Street?"

"Yeah, it's done the rounds. You really went for it," said a weary Craig.

"And everyone has seen it?" I asked.

"Most of Bedford I'd reckon."

"I just found it on YouTube," Graham said, before laughing hysterically. "You are totally naked! It looks like it was a very cold night, Adam."

"Craig, where did you buy that weight belt from? I might need it." I laughed.

"Honestly, Adam, this clip has made my year. You really do jump out of that bin," Graham said howling. He let his phone drift around the pub giving anyone and everyone a look.

"Thanks, guys, really, you saved my life," said Craig quietly into his glass.

"No need to thank us, we've all wanted to jump into the river at one point or another," said the all too matter of fact Graham.

"I was thinking we should start a lawn bowls team. Those old boys you see playing in the park, they look vulnerable. I think we can take 'em. I don't want to get ahead of myself but I think we could have a crack at the Olympics," I boldly stated.

"Worst case scenario we make the National finals. Count me in," cried Graham raising his glass.

Craig lifted his glass as well. "I'm down for that."

"Do you own a tracksuit, Craig? You're going to need to get one," I said throwing him my headband.

"Yes, you'll definitely need a tracksuit, but tell me, Craig, have you ever tried baking? Because earlier this year I took a pastry course and it changed my life…"

The three of us sat there for another hour laughing and crying, and at one point even singing. Graham offered Craig his spare bedroom and tomorrow we'll all go back to the hospital and see that he gets all the help he needs.

I walked in to our house just after ten. The kids were still up and bopping away playing a game of Limbo with Lucy and Judy in the new kitchen. They had no idea what I'd just been through and I wasn't about to tell them.

233

Hearing them giggle and watching them move care free, that was all I needed. I even took a second to admire Steve's handy work. By adding more cupboards he really did manage to make the room look bigger. What did I know?

It finally made sense as to why Lucy wanted to knock down the wall. It wasn't about being able to keep up with the Joneses and have the latest this or that, it was about carving out just enough space so that all of us could do exactly what we were doing, and that was dancing.